FALLING FROM THE SKY

FALLING
FROM THE
SKY

SARINA BOWEN

Tuxbury Publishing LLC

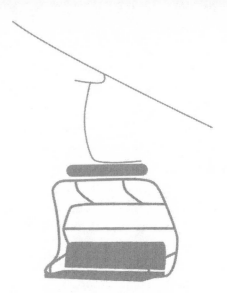

CHAPTER
ONE

STANDING on the snowy hillside under the December sun, Callie Anders found herself pulsing along with an unfamiliar bass line. The heavy groove scraping through the oversize speakers was the sound of bands she didn't recognize, played in clubs she'd never visited.

And it wasn't just the music. Nothing about the slopeside party resembled her ordinary life. The vibe felt more like an after-hours club than a sporting event. Beers in hand, spectators watched as a final competitor tipped his snowboard over the edge of the super pipe to drop into its steep curve. Gravity did its thing for the athlete, ramping up his speed as the board dropped into the valley of the pipe and then up the opposite side. At the top again, the guy snapped his hips upward, grabbed the board with one hand, and then whipped his body around in the air, reversing course to land neatly on the snow again. And then he was off, hurtling down the pipe with only seconds to prepare for his next trick.

Callie had seen snowboarding on TV, but in person it was even more impressive. After the kid launched his second trick

—some kind of dizzying spin, she lost count of his rotations—he seemed to meld his board onto the surface, his shoulders relaxing into a carefree stance as he dropped downhill again. As he sped by, Callie even saw his lips moving, forming the lyrics of the song thumping overhead.

After two more whirling tricks, he finished to a cheer from the crowd. The wool-clad heads in the crowd swiveled toward the giant screen, waiting for his scores.

"Not bad for a bunch of knuckle draggers," her friend Dane muttered beside her.

"I love it," Callie heard herself say. She was glad that Dane and Willow had towed her along to the snowboarding competition. "It's...half athleticism, half circus performance."

In response, Dane only snorted. And that made her best friend Willow grin. "He can't help it, Callie. A skier can't say anything nice about snowboarding. It's not in his DNA."

Dane gave Callie a wink. "In two months you'll see what a real mountain event looks like."

"I can't wait," she agreed. So far, she had only seen Dane race on television. But she'd already bought her plane ticket to Europe for the Olympics, where Dane would be contending for as many as four medals.

As if on cue, the music changed to the telltale trumpets of the Olympic anthem. Callie's eyes drifted to the big screen at the top of the pipe, which announced in giant type that the elite exhibition would happen next. After the last trumpet tone, the music devolved again into a heavy beat, and Callie saw the crowd begin to move with the music. As the knit hats and down jackets around her began to bob, it was as if Callie had been transported to a sunny, snowy land of hipsters. One that she wished she'd visited long ago.

Actually, she wished a lot of things.

When you spend nine years of your life becoming a doctor, there's a lot that you miss. For most of that time, the sacrifice hadn't really bothered her. But the past several months had been hard, and Callie had been spectacularly lonely.

It was almost exactly a year ago that she'd caught Nathan, her doctor boyfriend, cheating on her in an exam room with a leggy young nursing student. Callie had thrown the bastard out, of course. Yet twelve months later, Nathan and the nurse were still going strong, and she was still alone.

To make matters worse, Willow and Dane left Vermont for Utah in the spring, leaving Callie doubly bereft.

This weekend would make for a happy exception. Her friends were in town to take care of some business. And they'd brought Callie's new favorite person—their three-month-old daughter. Baby Finley was riding out the snowboarding event asleep inside Dane's ski jacket. If Callie put a hand on Dane's shoulder and raised herself up on tiptoe, she could just glimpse the baby's satin eyelids.

Callie hadn't seen her friends for ten weeks—not since she'd flown out to Salt Lake City after the baby was born in September. In the meantime, Willow and Dane had been busy settling into their new house, caring for the baby and surviving a whirlwind of preparations for the Olympic Games. In two months she'd see them again overseas. Callie and Willow would hole up in the hotel together, caring for Finley and cheering on Dane during the games.

It was all very exciting, but Callie still felt hollow inside. As she stood there beside her happy friends, she found herself fighting off unfamiliar feelings of envy. Willow had taken what seemed like an outrageous risk on a man with a difficult past. And now Willow was one third of what *Sports Illustrated* had recently described as "the cutest family in winter sports."

And what was Callie part of, exactly?

"So, you never told me," Willow said, stomping the snow off her boots. "Did you have drinks with the cute radiologist?"

"I think he's seeing someone," Callie answered without meeting Willow's eyes.

"Well, did you ask him?" Willow pressed.

"I'm pretty sure."

Willow shook her head, and let out an exaggerated sigh. "You know what I don't get about you?"

"Nope. But you're going to tell me whether I want to know or not, right?"

"I don't understand," Willow continued undeterred, "how you have the guts to literally restart someone's heart with a thousand volts of electricity. But you can't risk yours even to ask a guy out for drinks."

"Actually, we don't need a thousand volts anymore. The new defibrillators come in around three hundred."

"You're hopeless."

That was probably true.

"Hey, I see Hazardous!" Willow said, raising a hand to wave at someone.

Callie followed her friend's gaze over to the roped-off area at the base of the half-pipe. A very attractive man stood there, suited up for the snow, his helmet under one arm. The pose reminded Callie of old Apollo astronaut photos. When the guy spotted Willow, a lazy smile broke across his broad mouth, and he raised a hand in greeting.

"Let's go say hello," Willow prompted, angling through the crowd in his direction.

"After you," Dane said to Callie. And so she followed her friend toward the low fence.

"You've got to meet Hank Lazarus," Willow said over her

shoulder. "He parties a lot harder than we can keep up with these days, but the guy is seriously fun."

The closer they got, the more Callie stared. Willow's friend might be seriously fun, but he was also seriously hot. His shaved head was a military style that usually did nothing for Callie. But it was offset by big brown eyes and full, sensual lips. He was broad in a way that said "linebacker" more than "snowboarder," and his cut jaw and cleft chin were speckled with two or three days' worth of dark whiskers.

As they drew up to him, his chocolaty gaze took them all in. He lifted an eyebrow, and Callie saw that a barbell-shaped piercing bisected it. "Hey there," he said in a voice that was low and smoky. "What are you kids doing in Vermont?"

Sweet baby Jesus. Even his voice was hot.

Willow gave him a quick hug. "We're here to put my old farmhouse on the market. And Hank, this is my best friend, Callie. She's local."

Hank stuck out a hand, and Callie took it. As his hand engulfed hers, she felt her cheeks heat. His face was like the sun—too bright to look at directly. Hank gave her a quick head-to-toe, not even bothering to be subtle about it. And when he seemed to dismiss her out of hand, she wasn't even surprised. He was the sort of guy who existed in an alternate universe, far from beeping medical equipment and green hospital scrubs.

She was almost relieved when he let go of her hand and looked back up at Dane. "Where are we drinking later?"

But Dane hesitated, glancing toward Willow. "I'm not sure what our plans are."

First, the snowboarder's grin grew tight. "Holy fuck, Danger," he growled. "Seriously? You are so whipped that you can't agree to a beer tonight? Let me ask again. Where are we drinking later?"

Dane chuckled, and shook his head. "Chill, asshole. We need to make sure that the house we haven't seen in six months is still standing. Barring total destruction, I think a stop at Rupert's could work out."

As if she wanted a vote on the matter, baby Finley let out a squawk then. Dane bent his knees to bounce her gently, running one of his big hands soothingly under the bulge in his jacket.

Hank Lazarus watched his friend do this with a bemused expression on his face. "All right. Unless you get downvoted by the little family, Rupert's it is."

"Sounds good," Willow said. "Baby's first trip to the bar."

The snowboarder glanced uphill, toward the top of the pipe. "I'd better get a move on. Dane. Ladies." He gave them a sexy lift of his chin. "I'll see you later."

The very idea gave Callie a thrill. But of course she probably wouldn't be there. She was on call today, and that usually didn't end well. Even if she wasn't summoned to the hospital, she couldn't even have a drink like a grown-up.

Her life was pure glamour.

Not.

At least her pager hadn't gone off yet. The headliner event —the elite exhibition—was about to start. The music kicked up a decibel or two, and the champion snowboarders began to line up at the top of the pipe. Pictures of the elite athletes began to slide across the big screen overhead, shifting every few seconds in time with the music. The shots showed each man in street clothes, complete with stats and nicknames. Compared to the clean-cut skiers that Callie had met through Dane, these were the bad boys of winter sports. There were more goatees, ponytails, tattoos and piercings than a biker bar would boast. Not that Callie had spent much time around bikers, except when they landed in the hospital.

When Hank "Hazardous" Lazarus's picture popped up, Callie could only stare. In the photo, he was shirtless, and entirely droolworthy. He was all muscle, covered with ink. "Olympic Silver Medalist," the screen read.

"They say he's going to bring home the gold this time," Willow mused beside her.

But Callie wasn't interested in his stats. She was still admiring the man. He was sex on a snowboard, and so far out of her league it wasn't even funny. Even if she did show up for drinks tonight, if he tried to talk to her she'd probably swallow her tongue.

The screen flipped back to show the first man in the lineup, and then the crowd roared. Callie watched one of Hank's teammates take the pipe. And...wow. The aerial feats were on a completely different level than the competitors she'd seen before. The rotations were faster, and the tricks more complicated. And as soon as he finished, another boarder dropped into the pipe. Since there was no need to pause the action for judging, the exhibition was continuous. Callie's gaze became trancelike as the colorful bodies soared and twisted before her eyes.

And then Hank Lazarus's photo reappeared, and Hank came into view on the lip of the pipe, wearing his silver helmet and goggles. Callie stood up a little straighter as he dropped into position, his body in a loose, confident stance. At the opposite peak, he popped higher off the lip than seemed possible. With that big body tucked tight, he flipped backward with such casual finesse that Callie gasped. He landed the trick neatly, his shoulders bobbing with a cocky shrug.

"So that's what it's supposed to look like," Dane muttered. And it was true. The comparison between Hazardous and the others was stark.

He shot through the pipe again, and his next trick went so high, and with such whirling ease, that time seemed to stop as he hovered in the air. The rules of physics appeared not to apply to him. The crowd whooped when he landed, gliding at top speed through the gully.

Callie held her breath, wondering what miracle he'd pull off next. He launched again, grabbing the board in one hand and rotating through the air—once, twice and then a third time. The scenery seemed to change then, and it took Callie a split second to realize that the sun had gone behind a cloud. And just as she registered the phenomenon, something else happened. The snowboard smacked the lip of the pipe, instead of the snow on the slope below it. Since he'd achieved so much lift, the force of impact flexed the board, ricocheting the rider back into the air. Callie watched, helpless, as momentum yanked the man's body through space, propelling him head-first and at high speed toward the curving ice below.

And then his helmet hit the surface first. Hard.

Callie heard herself gasp. After a sickening bounce, his body slid down the ice into the center of the gully.

"Jesus Christ," Dane whispered.

People rushed onto the snow, a dozen of them quickly surrounding him.

Dane took a step forward, as if he wanted to run through the crowd to help. But Willow put a hand on his arm. "There are a lot of people down there," she said gently.

He just shook his head. "Get up, man."

But Hazardous lay crumpled and still.

Callie couldn't look away. In her head she heard the drumbeat of emergency procedure. Checking the vital signs, supporting his neck and back. But this time, it wasn't her job. At least three of the people down at the scene wore medical jackets. And even now she could hear the approach of ambulance sirens. On busy winter weekends, there was always a bus parked at the bottom of the ski-mountain access road.

"When you broke your leg," Willow said to Dane, "I'm sure it looked really bad from the stands."

But Dane just shook his head. "Christ. The Olympics."

From inside his jacket, the baby made a sound of protest. Dane tore his gaze away from the medical swarm and leaned inside to kiss her. Watching him, Callie's heart squeezed with some unnamed feeling of yearning.

"She's probably hungry," Willow said. "I'll take her inside and feed her."

Dane watched an ambulance thread toward the huddle on the ice, a look of unease still washing across his face. "I guess I'll come, too," he said.

Following them, Callie fingered her pager in her pocket. The odds of it going off today had just escalated. She pulled out her phone to check in.

"Busy?" she asked the triage nurse who answered the doctors' line. "If I were you, I'd pull up the call sheet for ortho and neuro. There was an injury during the snowboarding event at the ski mountain. You should be seeing them in fifteen minutes."

"Will you get called in?" Willow asked after Callie hung up. The ambulance was already threading its way out to the state road, its lights whirling.

"I'm not their first call," Callie said. "But give it an hour or two." Callie was a hospitalist—a doctor who kept track of admitted patients' medical needs.

"Okay," Willow said, her eyes on the retreating ambulance. "I guess Dane and I will go to the farmhouse now, and check things out. Then we'll swing by the hospital to try to learn what we can. We don't know him *all* that well, but..." She swallowed. "That looked bad, didn't it?"

"Yeah," Callie admitted. The force with which he'd hit the pipe was scary. "But bodies can be tougher than they look."

Willow shivered. "Can I call you in a couple of hours? No matter what, I want to see you tonight. Or tomorrow before we go."

"Absolutely. I need to hold that baby some more." She wanted that now more than ever, given the scary accident she'd just witnessed.

God, life was short. Maybe hers wasn't working out so badly, after all.

As it happened, Callie was not handed Hank Lazarus's chart until the following day. And even though she'd had twenty-four hours to process what she'd seen, the first sight of him in a hospital bed gutted her.

Pale and swollen from the IV fluids, he lay perfectly still. Since she'd last set eyes on him, he'd undergone an eight-hour spinal surgery. In place of the goggles and technical fabrics was a new sort of gear—tubes and monitors snaking from his body in every direction.

Even though he was sedated, Callie found herself holding her breath as she checked the tag on his IV bag. As his powerful chest rose and fell, Callie realized how limited her view of her patients usually was. Never before had she gotten such a shocking demonstration of "before" and "after." She met patients hours or days after things went sideways. But the ashen, broken man in room nineteen was such a frightening contrast to the one she'd seen drop into the half-pipe, it hurt her to look at him.

She forced herself to linger a moment longer. Though it shamed her to say it, there were times when she found herself judging the people in these beds. She might wonder why the patient had thought it was a good idea to ride that zip line so near to the trees, or drive so fast in the rain. Callie had always lived cautiously, and when she saw the results of a preventable accident, it seemed like such a waste.

But the memory of Hank Lazarus flipping effortlessly against the blue sky was burned in her brain. And in spite of the danger of it all, so cruelly proven by the sleeping figure in the bed, she didn't have to ask why he'd choose to take such a risk. She'd seen the power and the beauty of it with her own two eyes.

Beneath the sheet, he breathed. In and out. At that moment, there was nothing he needed from her. And nothing more she could do.

Dane and Willow tried to see Hank before they left again for Utah, but the first time they stopped by, he was in surgery. The second time, he was asleep. With the Olympics just weeks away, they had to go back to Dane's training. "Will you give him our love?" Willow asked, looking shaken in the waiting room.

"Of course," Callie answered, fully intending to do it.

As it happened, she never did.

In the first place, when Callie finally saw Hank conscious,

he didn't seem to remember her face. And this was not at all surprising. They'd only met for a second, and the mind often forgot the events just before a trauma.

And Hank had a distracting swirl of other visitors as the days went by. His parents, Callie learned, were a sort of Vermont royalty. They were part owners of the ski mountain. And Hank's father had built half of the condos in the county. There was a daughter, too, another athlete.

Callie gleaned many of these facts from the local paper, which ran a front-page story about Hank and his accident. At age eighteen, he'd left Vermont for the Rocky Mountains, where he'd taken a job as a dishwasher to pay for his lift tickets. He was as famous for partying as he was for winning competitions.

Reading about him made Callie feel like a stalker. But there it was in black and white, on the table in the break room.

From her chair beside Hank's bed, his mother was a silver-haired force of nature, barking orders at every nurse who dared to enter her son's room. And whenever Callie saw Mr. Lazarus in the hospital corridors, he was always on his phone

"They're flying in specialists. Three of them," nurse Trina told her. The nurse's station was another excellent source of news.

"That's a lot of firepower," Callie said.

"The Lazarus family can afford it. They gave a truckload of money to the hospital," she said, cracking her gum. "The pediatric wing built ten years ago? That was all them."

"Wow, really? You'd think their name would be over the door."

Trina shrugged. "They don't do bling. Mama Lazarus has those fancy shoes that no sane person wears in Vermont, right? And pearls? But no bling."

Callie had noticed that, too, actually. Even during this time of crisis, Hank's mother paced his room in camel-colored cashmere and suede. It was expensive, but not flashy.

"Their daughter survived some kind of childhood cancer," Trina continued. "They gave the money afterward as a thank-you."

"That's generous."

"Sure. But they're also exacting. That woman was on my ass tighter than a bumper sticker while I did his blood draw. Like I haven't been doing this for thirty years."

"It's because you look so young, Trina. She probably thought it was your first day."

The woman rolled her eyes, and Callie moved on to her next patient.

On Hank's third day at the hospital, a new visitor showed up. Outside Hank's room, seated on a plastic chair, wept a very pretty girl. Callie assumed this was Hank's sister. But again the nurses had the dirt. The statuesque blonde was the girlfriend, and a slalom skier. And a *model*. She even had a glamorous name: Alexis. Her only obvious flaw was temporary—she'd cried raccoon eyes onto herself each time Callie glimpsed her.

As Hank's medical coordinator, Callie was in and out, checking to be sure that the prescriptions his various specialists had ordered were appropriately dosed and would not conflict. She kept tabs on his vitals and watched for signs of infection. She was just one in a sea of faces caring for him.

It wasn't until the fifth day after his accident that they had a real conversation.

Outside the door to his room, his parents were engaged in

a heated conversation with a spinal specialist they'd whisked in from Cleveland. Callie slid past them to find Hank staring out the window. When he turned his head to meet her eyes, she could see that the post-surgical drug haze had lifted. In his gaze, she saw a man awake to the world, but in terrible pain. It was her job to try to figure out if that pain was something physical that she could relieve, or rather the distress of waking up to find he could not move his legs.

"Hi," Callie said softly. "I'm Doctor Anders. Or Callie, if you wish."

"Callie," he cleared his throat. "You look really familiar."

That wasn't what she had expected him to say. It would have been as good a time as any to mention that they'd met about ten minutes before his accident, but she couldn't bring herself to do it. Who would want to be reminded of that after-noon? "I've been here all week," she said instead. "But we don't expect you to keep track of the dozens of people who prod you all day."

"And all night," he added.

She sat down on a stool next to his bed. "That's my fault. I need to know that they're looking at your vitals every three hours. It helps *me* sleep." She winked, and was rewarded with half a smile. "Now, quick—before the room is invaded again by nurses' assistants—how's your pain? Is there anything you need?"

Hank lifted one hand to his face, and Callie was glad to see it. If his injury had happened farther up his spine, he wouldn't have been able to do that. With his palm, Hank rubbed several days' worth of whiskers, which only served to make him look more rugged, while he considered her question. "Let's see...I need a full rack of Curtis's ribs, with spicy sauce and a baked potato. And I need to get the hell out of this hospital."

She nodded obligingly, even though she couldn't fulfill any of those requests. But if he was talking about food and getting out of here, those were both good signs. "You'll be transferring to a rehab facility soon."

"Yeah," he sighed. His gaze wandered again, his eyes aiming at the window.

"The rehab place will let you sleep through the night," she said, keeping her voice light. "And you'll have your own clothes. I hear the food is better, too."

"Couldn't really be worse," he said, turning to face Callie again. His dark eyes locked onto hers, and Callie felt the moment stretch and take hold. He didn't say anything more, but he didn't have to. Silently, an understanding passed between them. It didn't matter if the food got better. Hank Lazarus was in for a shitty time, truly the shittiest time of his life. The distance he'd come these past five days was a descent from the highest high to the lowest low. And there wasn't a damned thing either of them could do about it.

"Hang in there," Callie whispered. "This right here is the very worst part."

He didn't break their staring contest. "You promise?" he rumbled, his voice pure whiskey and smoke.

But Callie didn't get a chance to answer, because his parents burst into the room then, both talking at the same time. "Forty percent chance that he'll walk from this guy, fifteen percent from the other?" Hank's mother bleated. "These people call themselves scientists?"

"Flew him all the way out here, and it's just more of the same," his father muttered.

Callie watched Hank's face close down as his parents approached.

"It's ridiculous," his father sputtered, pulling in a deep

breath in order to fuel the next phase of his rant. Meanwhile, Hank's jaw began to tick.

Callie stood up. "I know why you're frustrated," she announced, folding her arms. Hank's parents eyed her, and Callie knew what they saw—a young doctor at a good but rural hospital. And she wasn't even a specialist. But she had something important to say, and she wasn't going to let them stop her. "You need answers, and you need them now. I don't blame you at all."

Hank's mother opened her mouth to speak, but Callie cut her off. "Unfortunately, that's not how the spinal cord works. It doesn't care that you're desperate to know whether he'll walk again. There's swelling and bruising, and his body is still in shock. It's not the specialists' fault that they can't tell you what you need to know. The sooner you push for answers, the less accurate those answers will be, okay? Hank needs time, and we all need your patience. You won't have the answers for maybe a year. And no specialist, and no amount of money can change that."

Callie ceased her tirade to take a deep breath. God, she really shouldn't have added that last part. Never mention money to rich people. She expected Hank's parents to start yelling at her. But they didn't. His mother only began to blink rapidly with saddened eyes. And Hank's father wrapped his arms around her protectively.

"I'm sorry," she whispered into the silence. "If you'll excuse me." Callie took a couple of steps toward the door. On her way out, she turned to look once more at Hank. To her surprise, he winked at her.

Callie walked out, and spent the next few hours wondering if she'd receive a reprimand for raising her voice to the Lazarus family. But the call never came.

CHAPTER
TWO

NINE MONTHS LATER

AS HANK LAZARUS'S friend Bryan "Bear" Barry came in through the front door, he brought in the first cold draft of the season with him. Thankfully, he also came bearing a fresh bottle of tequila.

"'Sup, Hazardous?" Bear asked, shucking off his shoes.

Common wisdom said that autumn was Vermont's best season. But Hank wasn't feeling the love. He pressed mute on the TV remote control, and tossed it onto the coffee table. "The Patriots aren't on their game today." *And neither am I.* With a quick press of his arms, he transferred his ass from the sofa to the wheelchair, then wheeled after Bear to go around the bar and into the kitchen. He picked up the bottle where Bear had set it down. "Conmemorativo. That's the good shit. Are we celebrating something?"

"Maybe." Bear reached for a couple of shot glasses.

The bottle was cold to the touch, and once again Hank rued the end of summer. This past winter had passed in a hospital fog, and spring was a blur of rehab appointments. Summer had been bearable, what with the renovations to his house finally completed, and with the visits from his sister and his oldest friend.

But now winter would come again. Formerly his favorite season, now winter meant only dark days ahead. His friends would be back on the mountain, hurling themselves off cornices, trying to land a triple cork. Yet Hank would be here alone, in his new gimp pad. Doing what? Watching sports?

Fuck me, he thought. What was the point?

"Hazardous, let's do this right. Do you have any limes?" Bear was bent at the waist, staring into his refrigerator.

"They're over here, dude." Hank wheeled himself to the other end of the vast expanse of Vermont-slate countertop. He had no trouble reaching the fruit bowl, since his father's architect had redone the space with a tastefully terraced work surface, part at regular height and part a few inches lower, at wheelchair height. "Heads up."

When Bear turned, Hank lobbed the lime toward his burly, bearded friend. Then he opened a low cabinet—everything had been put in his reach—and pulled out a cutting board.

Bear hesitated over the lime, which he had been about to cut on the slate countertop. "Dude, your pad is more civilized than I'm used to." He put the lime on the board and finished the job.

"The gimp kitchen is the shit," Hank muttered. Too bad he would rather live in a double-wide with two functioning legs than in a castle for the broken.

"Where's the salt, then? Whip it out. And if you have any girls hidden around here, we could use those, too. Tequila tastes better when you're drinking it off a pair of D cups."

Hank grinned and plucked the salt off a turntable in the cabinet. There weren't any girls in his life, but Bear knew that.

Good old Bear. Without him, Hank would have been lost these past few months. It was Bear who made sure he got out of the house at least every few days, preferably for happy hour. And it was Bear who had sneaked half a dozen of those little airline bottles of scotch into the rehab hospital, where alcohol was not allowed.

Hank had drunk two of them while watching Dane win gold in the men's alpine giant slalom. And then he drank the rest while watching some Swedish asshole win gold in the men's snowboard half-pipe competition.

Bear sat down on a bar stool. "So now I'll tell you what we're drinking to tonight."

"Oh, I *know* what I'm drinking to."

His friend cocked an eyebrow but did not take the bait. "I have a big idea. I'm calling it 'Gravity Never Takes a Day Off.'"

Hank downed his shot and then bit a wedge of lime. "Bear, there's still no light bulb going on over my head, here. You'd better pour me another."

Bear only tented his hands on the countertop. "I want to make a feature-length snowboarding film. It should be a little bit of everything—some sick shots of big mountain heli-riding, some freestyle. Put it to some kickin' music. Like Warren Miller did for skiing, but edgier."

Hank didn't take his eyes off the bottle, which was still not headed his way. "Hasn't that been done before?"

Bear had forgotten about the tequila. "Not by us! You're going to be the face of the project. I can make a great film, but I need your cred."

That was laughable. "I don't have any cred. I'm a cripple. I have cripple cred." He stretched across the counter; the bottle was almost near enough.

"Listen, asshole." Bear held the bottle out of his reach. "You'll narrate it, and I guarantee we'll have a blast. Guys want to hear what you have to say about the amped-up stuff I'm going to film. And the ladies would throw their panties at the screen. You and I would get a couple of free heli trips to Alaskan peaks. What's not to love?"

Hank set down his shot glass with a thunk. "Let me get this straight. You would drag my ass to the top of some sick peak, and then wave goodbye on your board? Why would I bother, if I'm only taking the heli back down?"

Bear shook his head. "I'd be filming, not riding. And you don't have to come up in the 'copter if you don't want to. In fact, you can just do the post-production, if that's how you want to play it. But the partying is better in Alaska than in an editing room."

Hank just shook his head.

"Hazardous, I need you on this. I want to film it this season, and the first snowfall is only six weeks out. I'll edit next summer, and tour it a year from now. We can hit the college campuses, and enter part of the film in the Banff festival. It will be awesome." He put the bottle back down, and Hank snatched it.

He poured them each another shot. "Did you see the news?"

His friend's face became wary. "Which news?"

"Dude, don't play dumb. She's marrying a big mountain rider. That Canadian."

Bear shrugged. "So we won't use him in the film. That's easy."

That wasn't the problem, and Bear knew it. "She's *marrying* him, and it's only been eight months since she bailed on me." He downed his second tequila.

Bear moved the bottle away from him again. "She was a bitch, Hazardous. She was a bitch way before she blew you off. Okay? That is a bullet dodged. Let's not puke on her behalf tonight. She's not worth it."

Hank claimed the bottle again. Even if he suspected Bear was right, he felt the darkness hanging over him. "I'm not going to do the film. I appreciate the gesture, but you can offer it to someone who will really be the man."

"It's not a gesture, asshole. I want your face in this film."

"From the waist up, right?"

"It's a fucking *expression*. Moon the camera, for all I care. The women of the world are already wondering whether your ass is tattooed. Quit feeling sorry for yourself and let's make a great film."

"You're going to ride me, too? Nice."

Bear rolled his eyes. "Hazardous, you're not the only one who was ever disappointed, okay? We didn't make it. You and me both. I got cut from the team, and you crashed. But what are we going to do *now*?"

"I have absolutely no idea."

"My father wants me to take an accounting course." Bear tipped his head back and laughed at the ridiculousness of that idea. "You can join me as a pencil pusher. So *now* how does the film idea sound?"

Hank picked up the bottle. "I choose choice C—none of the above. And choice D—get very, very drunk."

Bear scowled. "Then lemme have one of those limes."

CHAPTER
THREE

CALLIE WAS SUPPOSED to be listening to her ex-boyfriend Nathan, who was describing a case. "He was unresponsive in the wee hours. His friend had to call in a bus. They pumped his stomach in the E.R., and I admitted him." As Nathan spoke, he shook his wrist, jiggling his watchband. That tic was familiar to Callie. He used to do it standing in their kitchen, drinking coffee after they made love.

Last month, Nathan's bottle-blonde nursing student had acquired both a nursing degree and a glittering diamond ring on her finger. This month, she began leaving copies of *Brides* and *Vermont Weddings* scattered around the break room.

It had been a year and three quarters since she and Nathan had broken up—but who was counting?—and here stood Callie, still alone. She was in a rut so deep she couldn't see over the sides.

"I have to run," Nathan said. "All you have to do is release him, okay?" He handed her the chart.

"Release him," Callie echoed. She watched Nathan walk

away, his white coat trailing behind. It wasn't that she was still desperate for Nathan. If she was honest with herself, their years together had never been all that passionate. But he was handsome, if a little bit nerdy. He was a successful doctor, with a nice smile. Most important, he'd been *hers.*

But she'd failed to keep him interested. And he'd proposed to a sorority girl with long legs and bleached hair. The betrayal still stung. It was almost as piercing as the other woman's overabundant perfume.

Callie tapped her fingers on the chart Nathan had handed her. She really needed to get away from this place. She loved Vermont, but it was not an easy place to be single. Last night, she'd spent the evening scanning medical career websites for positions in Northern California, near her parents. She could start fresh out there, and meet some more people her age. It just might work.

For now, she cast her eyes onto the patient file in her hands. *Male, Caucasian, 31 years old. Alcohol poisoning.* Then she saw the name. *HENRY (HANK) LAZARUS.* A nurse had scribbled *HAZARDOUS!* in the margin.

Hank did not want a serving of hospital mystery meat. He only wanted to go home.

"No thanks," he said for a second time to the buck-toothed woman who carried the tray into his room. Landing here last night had been an idiot move. As if Hank did not get enough of this place already. Three times a week he drove to the hospital for physical therapy sessions.

And for what? His body simply did not seem to want to relearn to walk. It didn't matter how many hours he spent staring down at his feet, willing them to move.

Before his accident, Hank's idea of paralysis had been informed by Hollywood. He'd assumed that a paralyzed man wouldn't be able to feel his legs, right? For some patients, that was supposedly true. But Hank had quite a bit of sensation in his legs. The pin-prick tests they liked to use on him were plenty uncomfortable, fuck you very much. He could feel his muscles about 75 percent as well as he'd felt them before.

He just couldn't *control* them anymore.

Meanwhile, the one-year anniversary of his accident loomed. Last winter he'd heard the phrase "it can take up to a year" stuck at the front of nearly every sentence that doctors said to him. It could take up to a year to figure out how much muscle strength he'd regain. It could take up to a year to regain mobility.

Now that nine of those months had passed, and Hank still wasn't walking, they didn't say it anymore. Now they started sentences with "every injury is different." Like little fucking snowflakes. He heard that line a lot these days.

Drinking himself into a stupor had been idiotic. But it wasn't like he didn't have a reason or ten.

"You gonna waste this food?" the orderly asked again, pulling Hank from his reverie.

"Someone else can have it," he answered. Someone with no taste buds. Someone who didn't have a mouth that was lined with wet newspaper, and a headache as sharp as his mother's opinions.

"Okay. If you're sure." The woman put the tray back on her cart and turned to go.

"Well, it says here..." came a sweet voice from the doorway, "...that Mr. Lazarus will only eat a full rack of ribs from Curtis's barbecue."

He looked up to see a very pretty woman in the doorway. Her honey-toned skin was set off by the white lab coat. Shiny caramel-colored hair covered up the name tag on her lapel, but he'd met this doctor before, he realized. She'd been here during the worst week of his life. As hazy and awful as those days had been, he couldn't forget the combination of such a perfect pink mouth with a pair of intelligent blue eyes.

"The chart stipulates spicy sauce and a baked potato," she added, stepping into the room.

"No shit?" He laughed. "That cannot be on my chart."

"I remember you, that's all." She winked. "I thought it was a perfectly sane thing to want." She flipped the folder closed and sat down on an ugly plastic chair next to the bed. "I'm Doctor Callie Anders." She held out her hand.

"One second," he said. Hank yanked his chair closer to the hospital bed and reached for the farther armrest. Leaning on it, he hiked his body off the bed and into the seat in one motion. Now he could face her properly. Even better, he looked like someone who was ready to leave the hospital. Already dressed in jeans and his sweater, all that was left was rolling out the door.

Then he shook Callie's hand, wondering how it was possible for anyone to look attractive under these godawful fluorescent lights. But the good doctor managed it. She had thick, wavy hair. Hank wanted to know how it would feel against his bare chest.

Right. Dream on, dude. He smiled at her. "You know, Doctor Callie, I happen to remember you, too. You're the one who told my family to chill the fuck out."

She grinned, revealing a dimple on one side. "Well, did they?"

"They did, for a little while. But now they're back on my case." *Shit.* He shouldn't be telling her any of this. He just needed to convince her that he wasn't going to drink another bottle of tequila, so that she would sign his release papers. And then he needed to get the fuck out of here.

She studied him, those blue eyes fixed on his. "What does your family want from you? Do I need to have another chat with them?"

"Nah," he shook his head. "They want me to try something called Functional Electrical Stimulation."

"Sounds kinky."

Caught off guard, he laughed. All the other doctors he'd met seemed to have had their sense of humor surgically removed. "If it was kinky, I might not object. It's a way of activating muscles that you can't use. It's a pie in the sky technology."

"But you don't think FES will work for you?" she asked. Her blue gaze became serious.

He shook his head. "After nine months, I still don't walk, and my family can't seem to get over it."

She flipped through the paperwork in her lap. "Your chart says you've made a lot of progress. You've regained a lot of sensation. You live independently. That's lucky."

Lucky. Hank hated that word. Since he'd woken up in the hospital room unable to move his legs, people kept telling him he was lucky to be alive. Most days, he felt anything but lucky. "Sure. But my family wants a miracle cure, or something. They're still waiting for my gold medal performance."

She looked up from the page. "That must be pretty depressing."

"Not all the time." He cleared his throat. "Dr. Callie, I know it's your job to clear me for release. Can you just set me free, if I promise not to come back again?" He was careful to look her straight in the eye. "I, ah…" He decided to tell her the truth, no matter how embarrassing. If he wanted out of here, he had to convince her that he hadn't been trying to off himself. "I found out yesterday that my ex-girlfriend is engaged to someone else. So I drank too much tequila. It was stupid, I admit. But I won't make a habit of it."

Dr. Callie actually flinched. "Ouch," she said, her features softening.

See that? Honesty really was the best policy.

"Although…" she hesitated. "The same thing happened to me just last month. And I didn't drink a bottle of tequila."

Oh, fuck. "Seriously?"

She nodded slowly.

"So what's your drug of choice?" he asked. Although, what Hank actually wanted to know was: what kind of douche would dump a beautiful doctor? Big brains and big tits in one convenient package. And with a sweet smile. Hank would bet any amount of money that Mr. Stupid was simply intimidated by her.

"Well, I got by with a whole lot of bad TV, and an embarrassing quantity of Ben & Jerry's. I gained five pounds, and lost five IQ points. But nobody had to pump my stomach."

Hank laughed. Hard. It was probably the first time he'd done so in weeks. It used to be a common thing for Hank to have an easy conversation with a woman. But that didn't happen anymore, and it was only partly because he spent so much time alone. Not everybody could see past the chair. But Callie had seen him looking far worse than this already. Plus, there was just no bullshit in her manner. Even now, her baby blues were studying him with an intensity that should have made him uncomfortable. But for some reason, he didn't want it to stop.

"Look," she said. But he was already looking, because she was easy on the eyes. Even with that lab coat covering her, he could see that she was stacked. A glimpse of the valley between her breasts was just barely visible. "There's no medical reason for me to keep you," she said. "I'm sure you know that. But help me feel better about not calling someone in psych. What was your intention?"

"To see the bottom of the bottle?" He lifted his chin. "Is that a trick question?"

"Hank, do you have suicidal thoughts?"

He swallowed. "No."

"That was an awfully long pause."

He rolled his eyes. "No, it wasn't. I'm not going to kill myself—it's really not my style. I was just drunk, Doc. If you institutionalized every drunk in Vermont, there'd be nobody left to make the maple syrup or operate the ski lifts."

He watched her pretty lips form a frown, while her eyelashes fluttered thoughtfully. "Hank, I'm uneasy for you. Is there anyone that you talk to about everything you've gone through this past year?"

"Thanks, Doc, but I'm not going to see a shrink. But if you're so worried about me, come and see me yourself."

"What?"

He hadn't planned to proposition her, because she didn't seem like the type to say yes. That, and he wasn't really in the market for female companionship. But old habits die hard. So he plunged onward. "Make a house call, Doc. Get away from the smell of bleach for a few hours. I'll cook you dinner."

Her eyes widened with surprise. "But..." A flash of

shyness crossed her pretty features. "You know I can't take you up on it. That would be unprofessional."

"Really? The minute I wheel out of here, I'm not your patient anymore. So what do you say?"

She licked those pink lips nervously. "I say…that if I were trying to distract a doctor from her line of questioning, asking her over for dinner would probably work most of the time."

He barked out a laugh. "But not all of the time?" Hank dropped his head with a defeated grin. Seriously, though, he had better get used to women turning him down. And what would a doctor want with him? She'd spent the last decade trying to cure cancer, or whatever. And he'd spent it getting wasted and tempting gravity to do its damnedest.

And then it had.

That grim thought made his stomach roll. But then he looked up to find Doctor Callie still watching him. And if he wasn't mistaken, a warm curiosity burned in her eyes. *Interesting.* Apparently, the good doctor liked some of what she saw. Unless his instincts were off. And probably they were. Because every other goddamned thing about him was off.

Truly, it didn't matter what Callie thought of him. Because Hank didn't have much to offer a woman. He was lonely as hell, but he was going to stay that way. Probably forever. He swallowed again, and steered his mind back to the matter at hand. "Sign my paper, Doc. I'll be a good boy."

She tapped the pen on her clipboard twice, and then she clicked her pen and signed the page. "Do me a favor and stay out of here, okay?"

"I'll do that," he said.

She slipped the release into his file, and then looked at him one more time. And somehow the moment lengthened, stretching out between them. Hank didn't know how long it lasted — probably for only a few seconds. But as they looked into each other's eyes, there was an energy there that Hank hadn't felt in a long time, and hadn't expected to feel again.

Getting ahold of himself, he did the necessary thing. He looked away. "Now, if you'll excuse me, I'm outie." He put his hands on his chair's wheels and propelled himself toward the door.

He felt her eyes on his back as he went.

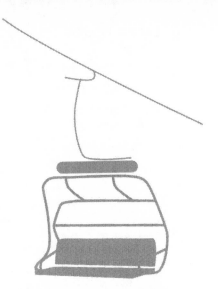

CHAPTER
FOUR

CALLIE THOUGHT about Hank Lazarus for the rest of her shift, and then every day for a week afterward. He was every bit as sexy as she remembered him. Even hung over, he had radiated testosterone, and a magnetism that left her wanting more. Sure, there was a sadness in his big brown eyes. That was to be expected. Yet here was a guy who had lost his entire career in one three-minute run down the half-pipe. And he could still flirt and laugh and make her feel fluttery inside.

She, on the other hand, had nothing but excellent health and a promising career. And still, she moved through her days feeling wooden and unhappy.

What the hell was wrong with her?

While she pondered this question again at the end of a long afternoon, nurse Trina waved her over to the triage desk. "Callie? Dr. Fennigan wants to see you in her office upstairs. She didn't say what it was about." The woman's face was filled with unguarded curiosity, and Callie didn't blame her.

Dr. Elisa Fennigan was the director of the hospital, and Callie had never been called onto the carpet before. She fingered the message slip between two fingers and tried to think. Could one of her patients be suing the hospital? It was always a risk. Every doctor got sued at some point, and they often didn't see it coming.

Crap.

She shoved the paper into her pocket on the way to the elevators. And when the car opened on the seventh floor, a receptionist looked up. "Doctor Anders?"

Callie nodded.

"Let me catch Dr. Fennigan before she hops on a call." She pressed a button on her phone. "Callie Anders is here."

"Send her in," said a pleasant voice.

The receptionist indicated an open door behind her, and Callie walked into the director's office.

Doctor Elisa Fennigan rose from behind her desk and held out her hand. "Callie, welcome. Please call me Elisa. I'm sure you're wondering why you're here. It's only for a good reason."

That was a relief. Callie felt herself relax as she shook Dr. Fennigan's hand. "It's a pleasure to meet you."

Dr. Fennigan—Elisa—sat down in her cushy leather chair. "Have a seat. Do you remember a patient by the name of Hank Lazarus? You saw him twice…"

Callie nodded. "Of course. Spinal cord injury sustained on a snowboard. He was admitted last week for alcohol poisoning."

The director nodded. "The hospital has an unusual opportunity concerning this patient. His parents are interested in a treatment called FES. Functional Electrical Stimulation."

"He mentioned that," she said. "He didn't sound convinced."

"Right," the director agreed. "But it's a promising therapy.

His parents are offering to fund a year-long study of it here at our hospital. We would open a therapy clinic for spinal-cord patients, including the FES technology, and run a trial to measure the effects of FES as a part of a traditional rehab program."

Callie's mind whirled. "So...at the end of a year, you would analyze whether the patients who did FES made greater gains than the others? But where would you get all those patients?" The Vermont and New Hampshire border was not the most populous place in the world, which was precisely why their hospital was not a hotbed of research activity.

"There are more spinal-cord injuries around here than you'd think," Dr. Fennigan said. "The V.A. hospital up in White River Junction sees most of them. Their patient pool includes injuries sustained in Iraq and Afghanistan. But intensive physical therapy is expensive. Patients will be willing to drive a few exits down the highway for a free program."

"I see," Callie said. "And we've got the space..."

Elisa nodded, her face solemn. The hospital had been shrinking a bit in the past few years, as paying patients became fewer and further between. "We have the space and the equipment. We even have a therapy pool, and it's underused. Facilities are not the issue."

"This is about money, right?" Callie asked.

Again the director nodded. "The Lazarus family is willing to spend more than a million dollars before this is over—that's on salaries, treatment and equipment. And we'd pull in grant funding for the study. It's a shot in the arm that the hospital sorely needs."

"That all sounds great," Callie hedged. "But what does it have to do with me?"

"Well, that is the unusual part. Hank Lazarus isn't wild to

participate. But he said he'd do it if you were in charge of the program."

Callie blinked back her surprise. "But I'm not a rehab specialist."

Elisa grinned. "He doesn't really care, apparently. And neither do I, quite frankly. Because your job would be to set up the program and administer the study. I'd put our therapy director in charge of working with the patients."

Callie didn't say anything for a moment. It was an amazing opportunity to work closely with the director of the hospital. But even so, her impulse was to refuse. Taking charge of something so far outside her field of expertise was a terrifying idea. "I've never administered a study," she said eventually.

"Callie," Elisa urged. "I'll bet you've *read* the finer points of several thousand medical studies."

"Of course." If you strung together the journal articles that Callie had read during the past ten years, the pages would circle the earth.

"Doctor, you could write this paper in your sleep. And I need you to do it."

"In my sleep?" Callie joked, and the director laughed.

"Preferably not." Elisa's face became serious again. "But I really must ask. Do you have any idea why Lazarus chose you?"

The question made her face feel hot. "No," Callie said quickly. The fact that she found Hank to be the most attractive man she'd ever met had nothing to do with it. "I don't know him, aside from his two hospital visits. When he was originally admitted for his injury, I did tell his parents to, as he put it, 'chill out.'"

Dr. Fennigan winced. "Was it a big scene?"

Callie shook her head. "Not at all. It was just one of those moments when he needed someone on his side. And apparently I was that person."

The director was quiet for a second. "Well, that's a bit complicated. Do you suppose the parents will hold it against you?"

"No way. Frankly, I'd be stunned if they remembered me."

Doctor Fennigan folded her hands on the blotter. "Okay, and that's been your only interaction with Mr. Lazarus?"

Callie's blush deepened. "I discharged him two days ago, and he invited me to have dinner with him. But I turned him down."

"Why?"

"Because he was my patient!" Callie stuttered.

"Not after you discharged him." The director looked thoughtful.

Stunned, Callie just shook her head. "Still. It wouldn't be right."

"So Hank Lazarus's motives are potentially complicated." Dr. Fennigan tapped the blotter on her desk. "Callie, am I putting you in a difficult position if you accept this job? If he harasses you, it won't be good for anyone. Not for you, not for the hospital..." She frowned.

"I don't think..." Callie sighed. "He doesn't strike me as the harassing type. Honestly, he was just being nice. I'd be surprised if he ever brought it up again."

There was a long silence while Dr. Fennigan thought it through. "Well, Callie," she finally said. "Let's go ahead with it, then. But I want you to feel free to come to me with the slightest problem, okay? If you need to bounce anything off me, my door is always open."

"Thank you," Callie said.

"This means you're getting a promotion. Your pay rank

will go up one grade, and I'm sure you'll be happy to hear that I'm pulling you from the hospitalist rotation for three months, while you get things up and running."

"Seriously? I won't be on call?"

Elisa shook her head. "Not unless you choose to do overtime. For twelve weeks, the study will be your full-time job."

Dr. Fennigan stood up. "It was a pleasure to meet you, Callie. Now, take these files. We have our first meeting with a representative of the Lazarus Family Foundation on Monday." They shook hands, and the director added a business card to the stack in Callie's hands. "My personal cell is on here. I mean it when I say to call me anytime. If you have any issues, we can't let them fester."

"I appreciate that," Callie said. Then she shook Elisa's hand again before walking back to the elevator, stunned. And when the doors opened again on the first floor, the first person she saw was Nathan.

"Hey, Callie," he said, thrusting a file at her. "Can you take this patient for me? Shelli and I have a dinner reservation."

Ordinarily, that sort of thing would ruin Callie's day. But this time, she caught the chart and gave Nathan an enormous smile.

"What?" he asked, clearly skeptical of her joy.

Callie had just realized the biggest perk to her unexpected promotion. For three months, she wouldn't have to work alongside Nathan. *Thank you, Hank Lazarus.* "I'm allowed to be happy, aren't I?" she teased. "Go on then. Do your dinner." She gave him another big smile and walked away.

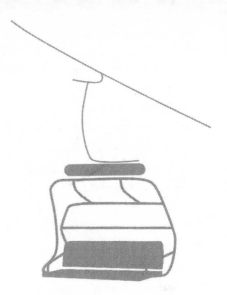

CHAPTER
FIVE

THE WEEKEND WAS JUST LONG ENOUGH to put Callie into a nervous tizzy. The study was a big opportunity for her. So she spent Saturday and Sunday reading every academic article she could find about FES. And Sunday night was devoted to a full-fledged fashion crisis. She tried on every scrap of clothing she owned. Twice.

Standing in the break room on Monday morning, Callie began to panic. There were three things that she feared in life: debt, failure and horror films. And this meeting with the Lazarus Foundation pushed two out of the three of her buttons. Running a clinical trial on a subject outside her expertise took Callie pretty far outside her comfort zone. And with a towering heap of student loans to repay, she couldn't afford to bungle this meeting and this opportunity.

Willow had given Callie a beautiful scarf one Christmas. She'd put it on today for good luck, and to complement her dove-gray suit. But as she stood in the break room fingering the delicate fabric with clammy hands, Callie was sure it looked all wrong. Removing the scarf, she matched up the corners one more time, draping the silk over one shoulder before retying the ends.

Tapping carefully into the corridor on heels, Callie ducked into the women's bathroom for one more reassuring glance in the mirror. But the reflection looking back at her was obviously trying too hard. She was still a poor kid from the wrong side of Sacramento who had studied medicine with deep financial aid. And she was still one screw-up away from potential bankruptcy. The scarf just looked awkward. Hank's elegant family would never be fooled by a piece of coral-colored silk.

Callie yanked the scarf over her head and carried it back to her locker. It was ridiculous, really. She could tie off a perfect surgeon's knot with a suture needle and tweezers. But she could not tie a scarf. There was no more time to wonder why. It was show time.

Carrying half a dozen copies of the presentation she'd prepared, Callie took the elevator up to the executive floor. "Dr. Anders?" Again, the receptionist greeted her, but this time it was with bad news. "Dr. Fennigan told me to tell you that her flight back from Bermuda was canceled. She's dreadfully sorry, but you'll have to do the Lazarus family meeting without her. I've set you up in the conference room, which is just to your left."

Callie tried not to let the panic show on her face. "Thank you," she whispered.

After a steadying breath, she walked into the conference room. There was just one person there, and Callie wondered if she was in the wrong room. The girl seated at the table was wearing slim jeans, hiking boots and a fleece vest over her T-shirt. It was the standard Vermont uniform. But Callie had been expecting a room full of suits.

"I'm Stella Lazarus," the girl said, rising to offer a hand to Callie. "Hank's sister."

"Ah, of course you are," Callie said, introducing herself. Stella's warm brown eyes were so much like her brother's. She was a tall girl in her mid-twenties, with shining dark hair. The Lazarus family produced only beautiful offspring.

Callie teetered nervously over to sit at the head of the table, wondering immediately whether that had been the right thing to do. She had no experience with corporate pomp and circumstance. And now there was a silence, and she realized she ought to fill it with small talk while they waited for the others. "It sure is nice out," she said. *Good one, Callie,* she chided herself. *The weather. How original.* She felt a drip of sweat roll down her back.

"Yeah, it's okay," Stella said with a glance toward the window. "In fact, I was hoping to go running before lunchtime."

"How far do you like to run?" Callie asked. Although she wasn't a runner herself, so this would be another conversational dead end. She sneaked what she hoped was a subtle glance at the clock over Stella's shoulder.

"Just seven miles," Stella said, with a less subtle glance at her own watch. "But it takes me about an hour, so..." She looked at Callie expectantly.

The moment stretched out in silence, giving Callie just enough time to worry whether she should have included the Scandinavian data in her presentation. Or whether that would have been overkill...

Stella cleared her throat. "The receptionist told me that Dr. Fennigan wasn't here today. So shouldn't we just get down to business?"

Callie just blinked at her. "I thought we were waiting

for..." She didn't finish the sentence, realizing at the last moment that Stella had just implied that nobody else from the foundation was coming.

"Hold up," the girl said, one palm in the air. "Were you expecting someone else? Don't I look like I belong at the grown-ups table?" Her dark eyebrows furrowed. "Sorry, I'm all you get. But don't worry—the checks won't bounce, even if the black sheep of the family writes them."

Callie opened her mouth and then closed it again. "I just..." She swallowed hard. This was awkward. "I just assumed that there were others who wanted to learn about FES. I know it's an interest of your mother's..." She scrambled to peel a copy of the presentation off the pile and slide it down the too-shiny conference table toward Stella. Sitting at the far end now seemed ridiculous. Her face heating, Callie got up and moved to the seat next to Miss Lazarus's. "Maybe we should start over. You can call me Callie, and I've been asked to run a therapy program testing the efficacy of FES." She extended her hand once more in Stella's direction.

Stella shook, but then crossed her arms over her chest. "My brother chose you to run the study, didn't he?"

"I, well..." It had taken only about five minutes for this young woman to turn her into a stuttering wreck. "He recommended me," she finished.

Stella grinned. "Of course he did. Hank always surrounds himself with beautiful women." She reached into a large handbag on her lap and pulled out what appeared to be a very big checkbook. "Let's just get this over with. What do we owe you for the set-up costs?" Stella clicked a pen into action, and then caught the look of confusion on Callie's face. "That's why I'm here, right? My daddy doesn't trust me to run my own life, but as long as I work for his company, and stay close to home, they let me run around with the checkbook."

By now, Callie knew she'd lost all control of both the encounter and the conversation. "Look, Stella, can I be blunt?"

"I don't see why not," she answered, crossing her arms. "I always am."

"Well, good. Because I've never been in the same room with a check larger than my mortgage payment. I didn't mean to insult you. It's just that I assumed that giving away a substantial amount of money took an entire committee, or something. Lawyers. Accountants. Maybe a note from the pope. I know how medicine works, I promise. But I don't have a clue about funding it."

For a second, Stella didn't blink. But then a slow smile began to tip up the corners of her mouth. And by the time it was complete, her eyes twinkled. "That's fair, I guess. Because I don't know a thing about medicine."

Callie let out a breath. "Then humor me for a few minutes, would you?" She'd come here today to do a professional job of explaining her study, and she would do that if it killed her. Callie patted the presentation on the tabletop. "I'd planned to tell you all about the project, because I think it's a great technology. It's exciting to me. Will you let me do that?"

Stella fanned the document with her thumb. "This is quite the doorstopper, Callie. Can you just give me the highlight reel?"

Cutting her losses, Callie flipped open her work to the third page, where there was a diagram of an FES bike. And then she explained it as best she could in sixty seconds flat.

"So," Stella said, tapping the page afterward. "The patient's muscles pedal a stationary bike without the brain's permission? That sounds so…science fiction."

"I know it does," Callie agreed. "But it *works*. And the hope is that the brain is listening—that we can remind the neurons how to fire intentionally."

"That *is* pretty cool," Stella agreed. "I can see how it would be a good workout, whether the brain gets on board or not."

"Exactly. But...*how* good? I want to quantify it. And then I want to prove to insurers that they should pay for it, because the patients they're covering will have lower health costs down the road."

Callie saw a light behind Stella's eyes. "Aha."

"Indeed."

Stella clicked her pen again. "Okay. So we're going to do some good in the world. I might hate my job, Callie, but I'm not a total bitch. How much should the first check cover?"

Callie took out an accounting statement that Dr. Fennigan had sent her and slid it across the table. While Stella wrote out the check, Callie's shoulders sagged with relief.

Three weeks later, the foundation's contribution had already transformed a portion of the hospital.

Callie skated into her new office, dropping an intake form for patient number thirty-eight into her already overflowing inbox. Her new job came with the luxury of an honest-to-God office, with a door on it. So what if it was the size of a large walk-in closet, with a window that looked out only on the hall-way? It was hers. It said so in gold letters on a placard outside the door.

The hospital had patched together a new suite of therapy rooms in record time, utilizing the space where the old daycare center used to be. Callie had assumed the construction would take weeks. But the dry wall guys and the painters had dropped in with the speed of paratroopers.

It was all just more evidence of the project's importance to the hospital. Terrified of letting Dr. Fennigan down, Callie had been working day and night to make sure the study launched smoothly.

Luckily, when she'd put out the call for study participants to nearby hospitals in Vermont and New Hampshire, she was quickly flooded with applications. Enrolling fifty healthy paralyzed participants was proving to be no trouble.

And interviewing the patients was proving to be even more fun than Callie had imagined it would be. As a hospitalist, she was used to working with sick people. But the applicants for her study were mostly healthy, active people. Most spinal-cord injuries happened to those between the ages of sixteen and thirty.

And three quarters of the time, the injuries happened to men.

So, Callie had spent the week taking baseline measurements of the muscles of healthy, active men. They had every body type, of course, and their injuries spread the gamut from lower leg paralysis to full on quadriplegia. But since the more mobile patients used their upper body strength all day long, a startling proportion of these guys were ripped and cut. Quite a few of them were ex-military, too. This meant that Callie had also spent the week trying not to blush as she wrapped the tape around sculpted biceps and triceps. More than once, she'd privately entertained the notion of creating a calendar of her favorites. She could title it *Hunks on Wheels*.

When Callie had spotted Nathan in the parking lot yesterday after work, he'd reminded her of a skinny mouse. Go figure.

"Hey, girlfriend."

Callie looked up to find her new coworker leaning his giant frame against her office door. "Tiny" Jones was a formidable creature. At six foot two, and about a thousand pounds of solid, cocoa-hued muscle, he was just as hunky as the applicants, and with a giant bubbly personality to go along with his big body. He held out a patient file, which Callie dropped into her inbox. "Another keeper?"

He nodded, and then tapped the clipboard under his arm. "And two more are waiting for us. Which of these two hotties do you want me to size up?"

Callie took the charts from his hands. One of them said LAZARUS, HENRY (HANK). "This one," Callie said, handing Hank's file to Tiny. She didn't think she could measure his body parts without bursting into flames. "But please ask Hank not to leave before I can pop in to say hello. You know who he is, right?"

"I heard that his mom and pop are paying our salary."

"More or less."

"So you're saying I shouldn't hit on him?" Tiny winked.

"Not right away," Callie teased. "Now, shoo. We're never going to eat lunch at this rate."

"Roger that. If you're going to take a minute with him, I'll swing by the caf. Turkey BLT and a coffee light?"

"Bless you. Let me just…" She fumbled for her purse.

"I'll put it on your tab." Tiny was gone before she could get to her wallet. The man was a godsend.

Fifteen minutes later, Callie found Hank waiting for her in the therapy room. "That guy is hysterical," he said by way of a greeting, jerking his thumb toward the door through which Tiny had just made his exit.

"Isn't he?" Callie agreed. "We're lucky to have him. A great therapist and a comedian, together in one extra-large package." She held out a hand to Hank, and they shook. But then Callie took a healthy two steps backward again, and not because Hank always made her feel like blushing. This past week she had noticed that standing back from a wheelchair patient made everyone more comfortable, as they didn't have to crane their neck upward to maintain eye contact. "How've you been?" Hank asked, folding his arms.

Callie tried not to stare at the tattoos emerging from under the sleeves of his skin-tight T-shirt, and snaking down his well-muscled forearms. He really rocked the bad-boy look. Not that she'd know anything about bad boys. She cleared her throat. "I've been great. And I wanted to thank you for recommending me for this job. I'm flattered."

Hank grinned. "Good. Because I want to flatter you."

Those teasing brown eyes were lit up and focused on her. Callie didn't know what to do with that sort of attention. "Um, there are a lot of people getting therapy who wouldn't be if your family hadn't stepped up."

Hank shrugged. "You'll have to thank my parents. I'm not that thoughtful of a guy. All I did was tell my folks that I wouldn't try FES if it meant relocating to Baltimore."

"Either way, I've read 5,000 pages about Functional Electrical Stimulation this month."

"Damn, girl. My apologies."

"That's okay, Hank. I have to say, after my nerdathon with the medical journals, FES does sound promising. It isn't an overnight miracle cure, of course. But the long-term benefits look very appealing."

"I'm sure it's nothing to sneeze at. But somehow I've just agreed to spend seven hours a week at the hospital, a place I'd do anything to escape. So tell me, doctor, how do you stand it?"

He still wore a smile, but it no longer reached his eyes. Callie dragged a chair over from against the wall and sat down. "Well, they pay me to come here. That helps."

"I'll give you that."

"To be honest, I don't feel like I'm at the hospital, lately. This is a therapy program, not a sick ward. Honestly, it's really fun to talk to healthy people for a change. They all have wheels like yours. But mostly, they're just getting on with life. I don't have to badger anyone about their meds, or call in a specialist."

Hank was quiet for a minute, his head tilted thoughtfully to the side, a muscle jumping in his masculine jaw. Callie could see him trying to decide whether or not to share whatever was on his mind. Then the most beautiful smile began tugging at his lips, traveling all the way to his eyes. "Well, if I have to come back to this place three times a week, I wanted to be sure to improve the scenery."

Callie felt her face heating. She would just have to teach herself not to be rattled by it. "So I guess you like our new paint colors, then? And the motivational posters?"

His eyes danced with humor. "Yeah. That's exactly what I meant. I'm feeling very motivated."

"Excellent." She looked down at the chart in her hands, in order to have somewhere neutral to put her eyes. "Then we'll see you next week. Tiny's going to whip you into shape."

"I like to do my own whipping."

Callie rolled her eyes at him. "I'll bet."

Hank chuckled, then popped a wheelie in his chair. "Later, Dr. Callie."

"Later," she echoed as he went out the door. *Don't stare*, she reminded herself, dragging her eyes away. The flirting always rattled her. The minute that chocolate gaze landed on her, she got a little light-headed. But that was just Hank's way. He flirted his way out of trouble. And she was just going to have to learn to control her reaction to him.

CHAPTER
SIX

THE FOLLOWING MONDAY, Hank had his first two therapy sessions. First up was a stint in the FES room, where he was hooked by electrodes to a stationary bike, the wires instructing his legs to pedal. It was unsettling, if not uncomfortable. Hank jammed his ear buds in his ears, turning up the volume of the Red Hot Chili Peppers, and drowning out any irrational feelings of hope. After FES, Hank had a half-hour break. He bought OJ from a vending machine outside the locker room, and changed into his swim trunks. Of all the therapies on the roster, aquatherapy sounded like the most trouble and the least fun.

Unfortunately, meeting the aqua trainer did not change his opinion.

"Righty-O! We're going to work on hip mobility today!" The chirpy aqua trainer slapped one fist into the palm of his hand and urged Hank to get into the pool.

Righty-O? Hank was not feeling the love. He did not want to get into the pool, especially with this clown. "We are, huh?" was his growled response. He knew he sounded like a belligerent bull. It's just that every time this idiot smiled, he couldn't think of any reason he should cooperate.

"Come on, then!" the trainer tried again. "Let's get wet!" He was a skinny dude with floppy blond hair and red swim trunks. He looked like an overexcited lifeguard, and with a voice so eager that it made Hank's teeth hurt just to hear it.

Hank took another pull from his juice. "Suppose we don't and say we did?" He wasn't in the mood to swim, or to be hitched like a mule to an underwater treadmill. He didn't even think he could summon the will to go through the motions.

Bay Watch dude sighed. "If you blow off this hour of therapy, you'll just have to reschedule it."

Who agreed to this crap, anyway? Oh, right. That would be him. He'd let his mother bully him into it. Everyone thought the Lazarus family was so generous, but Hank saw his parents' actions for what they really were—manipulation. Forty-nine other people's treatment depended on whether Hank got into the pool or not.

Damn. His legs might be useless, but that didn't mean he enjoyed donating his body to science.

"Good morning!"

Hank turned automatically toward the merry voice coming in through the pool door. And when he did, he was rewarded with a unique view of the lovely Doctor Callie. Today she was uncharacteristically dressed in a pair of bright pink running shorts and a close-fitting athletic top. Even better, her face was flushed in exactly the way he imagined she'd look after she'd been...

Hank gritted his teeth. Wasn't he just all about the self-torture today?

"Good morning," the chirpy trainer replied to his pretty boss. "Are you here to work out with us?"

"No, but I've just been Functionally Electrically Stimulated," Callie announced.

"Oh, baby," Hank said. He felt his mood lift, as it always did when she walked into the room.

She came closer and gave his upper arm a playful slap. "Mind out of the gutter, Hazardous."

He grinned. "You let them hook you up to the Franken-machine?"

"Well, *sure*. I'm not going to write a study paper about a therapy that I'm not willing to try. And it didn't hurt. It was just a little creepy watching my legs push the bike pedals without any help from me."

"Welcome to my world," Hank said, finishing his juice. It *was* creepy. But he had to admit that the FES bike had been a decent cardio workout. "Shouldn't you two be in that pool by now?" Callie asked, eying the aqua trainer.

"Nothing would make me happier," Mr. Chirpy replied.

Hank grunted. "Shit, you don't waste any time throwing me under the bus."

"Yeah, because this is definitely my fault," the little prick shot back.

"Guys? Is something the matter?" Callie asked, looking between them.

Hank shook his head. "Just don't feel like being strong-armed. That's all."

"Hang on," Callie crossed her arms over her generous bust, which only served to improve his view of her cleavage. "Who do you think is strong-arming you, Hank? You're here on your own accord."

As if. "Right. Then I'll leave on my own accord." The grumpy-ass statements would just not stop rolling out of his mouth.

"And that doesn't leave us in the lurch at all." Callie tipped her head toward the trainer. "Jerry, would you give us the room?"

After Mr. Chirpy left, Hank looked up at Callie, feeling sheepish. "What?"

"You tell me."

"I'm just not feeling it today. This bullshit won't change me."

"How can you be sure?"

"Because it won't, okay? Aquatherapy is not going to make me walk."

"You could be right. But why would you assume there'd be no benefit at all?"

There was no way to make her understand, and arguing only made him sound like a whiner. "Life jerks me around, Callie. Today, I'm just sick of it."

"I don't jerk you around. You're going to build muscle and reduce spasticity. You're an *athlete*, Hank. You of all people should understand the value of a marginal change. The difference between a podium finish and fifteenth place."

God, she was too smart for her own good. Everything she said made sense, except for one word. *Was*, he wanted to correct her. He *was* an athlete. Past tense.

Thinking about all this shit just made him tired. "In the meantime, you want me to put on my happy face and perform like a hamster on its wheel. In the waiting room, you've even got those photos on the wall—the ones with the slogans about will and determination."

Callie smiled slowly. "Those are pretty awful, aren't they? My favorite is the picture of the baby walking. *The journey of a thousand miles begins with one step.*"

Hank snorted. "Not the one with the eagle? *Dare to soar?*"

"Nobody expects you to flap across the Grand Canyon, Hank. But I do need you to get in the damn pool. If you were so set against participating, why did you rope me in?"

Fair question. Hank realized that he had two choices. He could argue with Callie, which would only make him feel worse. Or he could capitulate.

It was an easy choice.

He yanked his T-shirt over his head and jammed it into the bag that hung behind the seat of his chair. When he turned to Callie again, her eyes were wide. If he wasn't mistaken, a certain pretty doctor was having a wee bit of trouble keeping her eyes off the ink on his chest.

That was a happy thought. He wasn't dead yet.

Hank pressed his body up out of his chair, twisted his torso and lowered himself onto the pool deck with as much grace as he could manage. "You mean, why did I rope you into this study? Here—come sit."

Callie toed off her sneakers and socks. "Look, I'm happy to get the promotion. Don't get me wrong." She tested the edge of the pool deck for dryness. Then she sat down next to him, her feet in the water.

"You must think I'm the biggest pain in the ass," he said, leaning back on his hands. He saw her eyes dart down to his abs and then back up again. As he watched, she took a careful breath and focused her gaze on his face.

He bit back a smile. "My family convinced me that the study was a good idea, but some days I just don't feel like being somebody's lab rat." He tipped his head to look at her. "But you never make me feel that way, Callie. You always talk to me and not the chair. The first time you ever walked into my hospital room, I noticed that." It was all true, but he needed to shut up now, that was for damned sure.

Hank leaned forward and felt the water with his hand, even though his feet were already in it. But his feet weren't as helpful as they used to be. "Warm, isn't it?" Then, without waiting for an answer, he tucked his chin and ducked forward, rolling face-first into the water.

When he broke the surface again, Callie was shaking her head at him, a smile on her face. "The sign says no diving," she pointed out cattily.

He rolled onto his back. "I never was one to follow rules."

"You know why they post No Diving signs, right?" She reached forward, put the tips of her fingers below the surface and splashed water in his direction.

He chuckled. "We wouldn't want anyone to *break his back.*" At this bit of trenches humor, Callie only smiled wider. God, she had a beautiful smile, and her eyes danced whenever she teased him.

Hank rolled again and began to tread water. It was hard work without the use of his legs. But he'd be damned if he was going to wear one of the float belts like they wanted him to. Those were for pussies. With something like a breaststroke, he swam forward toward the pool wall. "Callie?"

"Yes?"

Instead of answering, he reached up for her hands and pulled. With a shriek of surprise, Callie plunged into the warm water beside him.

She came up sputtering. "Asshole!" was the first thing she said.

He laughed, treading water in front of her. "That's not very professional language."

"Well...jeez." She splashed him again, then found her footing on the pool floor. She was standing neck deep in the water.

Hank was still treading water, and probably not making it look easy. Callie held out her hands to him. It was probably a simple reflex on her part, but he would take what he could get. He grasped her forearms gently, letting his natural buoyancy do the rest of the work. "But how was it fair that I had to get into the pool and you didn't?"

"You're wearing a *bathing suit*, for starters." Her voice dropped and her eyes grew huge, as if she had just become very conscious of how close together they were now.

"That's a minor detail," he whispered. Callie's wide-eyed gaze reminded him of a skittish kitten, and he didn't want to scare her off.

"Thank God I have work clothes in my office," she said, giving her lips a nervous lick.

"Thank God," he echoed. And then the temptation was just too great. He bent his elbows, which caused his body to float toward her. Closing the distance between them, he gave her a single, slow kiss. Her breath hitched in surprise, but her lips were moist and sweet.

For a fraction of a second, he hesitated, waiting for her rejection. But...*fuck it*. How many months had it been since he'd kissed a beautiful woman? And when was the last time he'd met someone as great as Callie? Maybe never. He was just going to assume that he hadn't read the signs wrong. And if it blew up in his face, he'd deal with that later.

"Mmm," he hummed against her lips. He kissed her again, lingering this time, his lips a slow sweep against hers. Just when he became convinced that she wouldn't respond, he felt her mouth soften under his, her face slanting to get closer. With a quiet little gasp, she opened up to him. He pulled her nearer to his body, deepening the kiss. The morning's frustrations fell away, until there was nothing but the gentle slide of her cautious tongue against his, and the warm water lapping against his body. Heaven.

Unfortunately, Callie's brain seemed to flicker back online before he was ready to let her go. She stiffened slightly and began to pull away. He nipped her bottom lip before she could escape, and received a breathy little groan in response.

Even so, she ended the kiss. "Someone will see," she whispered.

"Sorry," he breathed. "But I really like you, Callie." He stretched forward until his mouth was beside her ear. "I'm sorry I got you all wet. Although I'd like to get you even wetter."

Her response was the deepest blush he'd ever seen on a girl. "God, you're going to get me fired." She pushed his arms back to a respectable distance.

But he felt no real remorse. Kissing Callie had felt so damn good. Though he had to let her go, since she'd asked. So Hank swam over to the side of the pool and hoisted himself out. Twisting his torso, he managed to get his butt onto the pool deck. "Let me get you a towel," he said. "It's the least I can do." He maneuvered himself back into his wheelchair, twisting once again to get his ass into the seat. Then he wheeled over to the towels stacked in the corner, grabbing three.

Callie gratefully accepted two of them. "My office door is only fifty feet from here. I wonder how many coworkers I'll run into on the way?" She climbed out of the pool and wrapped a towel around her midsection.

"That's me on a good day," Hank said.

"What do you mean?" Callie squeezed water from the ends of her hair, and Hank tried not to stare at the way the thin nylon of her running shorts had pasted itself to her body.

He shouldn't have brought it up, because now he had to

answer the question. "Everywhere I go, I'm the guy who looks wrong. Wheels instead of feet..."

Callie frowned, and he could see her marshaling some kind of argument against that logic, but he didn't want their conversation to go there.

"Listen, lady. I want to see more of you. If you'll let me."

That shut her up, and quick. First he was rewarded with a smile, but almost immediately she began to look sad. "I don't know if I can do that. The ethics are messy."

"You're not my doctor, Callie."

"That's true, but..." The door opened then, and her eyes went wide. And they weren't even near one another. The girl was going to be seriously uptight about this. He had his work cut out for him.

"What happened?" chirped the aqua trainer guy. *Shit.* Hank had managed to forget that man existed for a good ten minutes.

"She fell in," Hank said.

Callie's laugh was like music. "I fell in when you *pulled* me in."

The trainer had a laugh like a hyena, but at least Callie didn't look embarrassed anymore.

"Dude, can you grab her clothes?" Hank asked, to get rid of him. "They're in her office."

"The duffel on my chair," Callie added quickly. "I'll owe you one."

"Not a problem," the trainer said, hoofing it out of the room on his perfectly white sneakers.

"I mean it," Hank said as the door swung shut. "Let me make you dinner."

She looked over her shoulder toward the doors, with that

nervous-kitten look on her face again. "We'll talk about it another time," she said.

"Sure," he agreed, even though her brush-off wasn't the best sign. But he'd figure something out, some way to catch her off guard. If he could figure out a way to spend time with her somewhere other than the hospital, that would help.

At least now he had something fun to think about while he swam with Mr. Chirpy.

The next day, after a therapy session, Hank wheeled toward his locker. There was a half sheet of paper taped there, and as he approached, it appeared to be another one of those cheesy motivational posters. It had the same black border and dramatic text. "MOTIVATION," it read, underneath a photo of a rock climber high on a mountain peak, the sun setting brilliantly behind him. Below that, in smaller text, he read: "If a picture and a perky saying are all it takes to cheer you, then you probably have an easy job. The kind that will be outsourced to India."

Hank pulled the picture off his locker and smiled to himself. Callie was *flirting* with him.

Game on.

CHAPTER SEVEN

FOR THE NEXT SEVERAL DAYS, Callie could not stop thinking about Hank's kiss. She walked in a fog, just remembering those few minutes of bliss. If not for the pool water, Callie might have actually burst into flames in his arms. She had never been kissed by anyone even half as sexy as Hank Lazarus. He had sinfully full lips, and thick, dark eyelashes that ought to be illegal on a man. The guy was practically bursting with testosterone, and seemed to have the sort of permanent five o'clock shadow that proved it. And the man could kiss like...she didn't even have a basis for comparison.

In a weak moment, she'd left him that satirical poster, and had then been honestly relieved that he hadn't mentioned it since. And yearning for Hazardous was futile. In the first place, he would never go for the geeky doctor type. And second, he was a patient in her program. She couldn't even name a less appropriate target for her lust.

But those broad, inked shoulders...

Crap. She was going to make herself insane. And just the possibility that he might be even a little bit attracted to her meant that she would not be able to set it aside, even though she should.

When Sunday came around again, Callie was alone. As usual. But at least she wasn't working. Instead, she drove to Willow's farmhouse to do a favor for her friend. Pulling up the long driveway, she passed the FOR SALE sign on the lawn. She killed the engine in front of Willow's garage, and got out of the car.

Before, when Willow had lived here, the cheerful cluck of a couple dozen chickens had always greeted her when she arrived. But they'd been given away to other farms when Willow left Vermont. Now it was depressingly quiet.

Callie had offered to swing by the unsold house just to make sure that nothing had gone wrong in the months since Willow and Dane had last seen it. Circling the exterior, every-thing looked fine. So she took Willow's key out of her pocket and let herself into the house.

Because it was such a pretty October day, she left the kitchen door open while she worked. The old farmhouse needed airing out. The kitchen looked dusty, so Callie damp-ened a dishtowel and began to sweep the surfaces.

She had to admit that seeing the place so lifeless made her sad. She and Willow had eaten countless meals at this old wooden table, sipping wine and lamenting the lack of avail-able men in Vermont. Now Willow was off with her very own mountain man, and Callie was still alone. But just as she draped the damp dishcloth over the oven handle, her pocket-book began to beep.

She still carried a pager since cell phone service could be

unreliable in rural areas. The number on the display was unfamiliar, which probably meant that someone had misdialed. But she picked up Willow's phone and called just to be sure. When a man's voice answered, she said, "This is Doctor Callie Anders, and I was just paged?"

"Doctor Anders, where are you?"

The warm, husky sound of his voice made her heart speed up. "Hank?"

"Yes ma'am."

"Ouch," she laughed. "My *mother* is a 'ma'am.' How did you get my pager number?"

"The nurses at the hospital like me."

Of course they did.

"*Miss,*" Hank tried again, "may I inquire of your whereabouts on this lovely afternoon?"

Her heart rate doubled at the idea that Hank wanted to see her. "Well…I was just checking up on my friend's vacant house. And now I'm about to go outside and pick apples."

"So where is this paradise?"

"On North Hill. Why? Are you going to help me?"

"You have me thinking about apple pie now."

"I'm not much of a baker."

"That's okay. Where am I headed?"

Before she could talk herself out of it, Callie gave him Willow's address.

Twenty minutes later, Callie watched from the back meadow as Hank's macho car crested the top of Willow's gravel driveway.

When she'd first seen the cherry-red coupe in the hospital

parking lot, she'd imagined that Hank was the only one in the world who put custom hand controls on a Porsche. But now that she'd gotten to know some of the study participants, she understood her mistake. There were plenty of people in the world interested in driving sports cars without the use of their feet. The paraplegic men in her study loved to talk about their cars, just like any bunch of men anywhere. She found herself repeatedly learning the same lesson from these guys: except for their disproportionate upper-body strength, they were just like everyone else.

The driver's door opened, but it took Hank a couple minutes to assemble his wheelchair. Callie suppressed the urge to cross the grass to greet him. She'd never put a chair together before, and would be no help. But also, Hank just wasn't the type of guy who wanted to be fussed over.

She waited until he was rolling toward her to hop down from the three-foot ladder she'd found in Willow's shed. Callie rubbed one of the apples she'd picked on her jeans and took a bite. It was sour enough to make her pucker.

"That good, huh?" he asked, a big smile on his face.

"I think these are pie apples," she said.

He held out one hand, exposing a riot of ink on his inner arm that crept up from his sturdy wrist into his T-shirt sleeve. "Let me taste."

She handed him the bitten apple and he took a big bite. His eyes rolled back in his head with pleasure. "Wow. These are great." He looked up into the branches of the tree. "And your friend has taken good care of this place. Check out that pruning."

Callie realized it was high time to mention their common friends. "Hank, have you been here before? This is Willow's house. I believe you know her."

He looked up quickly. "As in *Danger* and Willow?"

Callie nodded. "Willow is my best friend. This is her farmhouse—they've been trying to sell it since last winter."

Hank's gaze traveled to the white clapboards of Willow's house and then back to Callie. "I think I remember something about that." He took another bite of the apple and frowned.

Callie said nothing, hoping she hadn't shaken loose any memories of the day of his accident. "They have a nibble on the house, so Willow asked me to come by and air it out."

Hank laughed. "What? Dane couldn't chip a little corner off one of his gold medals to pay for someone to do his housework?"

"I don't mind helping them."

His dark eyes measured her warmly. "I'm kidding. Some things you just need a friend to do for you, right?"

Callie didn't answer him right away, because she'd slipped into the spell of his chocolate gaze. "Right." She cleared her throat.

"...And there's apples in the bargain. How many did you get?"

She showed him the dozen or so in the basket.

"That's a good haul. And it reminds me—I should get this butter out of the sun." He patted the duffel bag on his lap.

"Butter?"

"For the pie."

She laughed. "You aren't fooling around."

"Callie," he grinned, "I am *always* fooling around."

The sexy quirk of his full lips was so potent that it was all she could do not to tip forward into his lap. She'd replayed their kiss in her mind so many times that his mouth seemed to have a magnetic pull on her. She hoped he didn't notice that she was staring.

Just then, an apple landed at Callie's foot with a plop, distracting her. She bent over and picked it up. "Oh, God, look!" she said, turning the apple to show Hank. There were fresh bites out of it, where the snowy apple flesh was still glistening.

Hank looked up into the tree, and then pointed.

A gray squirrel sat on a limb directly overhead. As Callie watched, he began to chatter and complain.

She laughed. "I think he just said, 'You bitch! That's mine!'" Callie replaced the apple on the grass, and then looked up at the squirrel. "It's all yours. We're out of here."

Callie led the way into Willow's kitchen. But it took Hank several tries to mount the old stone stoop and wooden threshold. It occurred to Callie that until now, she'd only observed her study participants atop the wide, level hospital floors. She hadn't stopped to realize that the rest of Vermont was probably far less passable. They lived in the land of ancient doorjambs and creaky floorboards.

He had mentioned before that his father had renovated Hank's home after the accident. But surely most of the other study participants weren't so lucky.

"Nice place," Hank said, taking in the white kitchen cabinets and the overstuffed furniture on the opposite end of the room.

"Isn't it cool? We had some good times in this kitchen. Willow was the cook, of course. My job was usually just pouring the wine."

"Somebody has to do it," Hank said. Then he pointed up to a shelf above Willow's old fireplace. "What's that?"

"A very strange violin. It's pretty, but it's in really bad shape."

"Can I see it?"

"Well, sure." Callie crossed to the hearth and stood on tiptoe. The old leather case had a coating of dust. She picked up the damp cloth she'd been using and swiped it clean. "This came with the house. Willow never knew what to do with it."

She handed the case to Hank, who laid it on his lap. Carefully, he snapped the clasp open and lifted the lid. A velvet cutout lay atop the violin. Pushing this aside, Hank removed the old instrument from its case. "Damn, it's a Hardanger. Look at all this inlay work." He ran a finger over the designs worked into the wood. Picking up the instrument, he held its face up to his own, tilting it back and forth, peering through the f-holes. "Huh," he grunted. He plucked at the strings one at a time with his thumbnail. With the care of someone diffusing a bomb, he began to tweak the tuning pegs, plucking the strings at intervals to test them. "The bow is shredded. That's a shame."

Hank tucked the violin under his chin and began to pluck out a tune. It only took Callie a second to identify it. He was playing "Oh! Susanna." She hadn't heard that song since she was a kid, when her grandfather used to sing it. *Well it rained all night, the day I left...*

Hank only played for a minute or so. But by the time the last note was ringing in the air, her jaw had fallen open. "Wow. You play the violin?"

He shrugged. "Used to." He tucked the instrument back into the case. "Do you think Willow would mind if I had a luthier in Montpelier look at this for her? I think it's an antique." His thumb massaged a line of stitching on the leather case.

"Take it. She won't mind at all."

Hank tucked the violin into the mesh bag on the back of his chair. "Well," he said. "We'd better preheat the oven." He rolled to Willow's range and fiddled with the digital display.

And then, after he'd dazzled her with his hidden musical skills, Hank proceeded to *bake.*

"We don't have any ingredients," she argued at first.

"I brought flour, sugar and butter," Hank said, pulling them out of his pack. "But if there's any salt and cinnamon in those cupboards, this will taste even better." He positioned himself sideways to Willow's sink, turning on the tap. "And we'll need a few drops of cold water. Can you scare up a mixing bowl from somewhere?"

Callie opened Willow's pantry and began to pick through her spices. "Go slow. I'm still looking for cinnamon. Found it!" She smiled to herself. It had been a while since she'd had an unpredictable weekend like this. Even if she was about to be exposed as someone who could barely boil water, this was much more fun than sitting on the couch in her condo with a fresh stack of medical research articles in her lap.

As soon as Callie found a bowl and a knife, Hank poured in a heap of flour, and then began to cutting bits of butter into it.

"You didn't measure that," Callie pointed out.

"It's about a cup and a half."

"*Okay…*" She was in the presence of greatness. A hot man who baked pies from scratch? "Wait…what about a pie dish?"

He shrugged. "If we don't have that, a cookie sheet will do. This is going to be a rustic apple tart. Oh—and we need something to roll out the dough. If there's no rolling pin, I'll use a bottle."

She laughed. "MacGyver bakes."

He rolled up his sleeves and began to knead the butter into the flour. She peeled and sliced the apples, all the while thinking warm, fuzzy thoughts about his muscular forearms as he worked. Callie practically needed to fan herself just watching him. She tore her gaze away, redirecting it to the apples she was supposed to be peeling.

When the dough was formed, Hank flattened it into a disc, then spread flour on Willow's wooden work table. With a rolling pin and about ten seconds of effort, he had a pretty butter-yellow crust, which he transferred to a baking sheet. "Let's toss some cinnamon and sugar on those apples..." he said, taking the bowl from Callie. "You have plenty here." With another careless sprinkle of ingredients, he piled the seasoned apples into the center of the crust, then crimped the edges around to encircle them.

"Wow," Callie said appreciatively. "That's beautiful." She shook her head. "You and Willow. She's one of those super competent ninja people, too, and she totally downplays it. 'Oh, I have no useful place in the world. But let me serve you the bread I baked from the wheat I grew.'"

Hank snorted. "And here I was feeling like a loser because I can't reach the oven timer." He pointed to an old-fashioned timer on a shelf above the sink. "Could you set that thing for forty minutes?"

Even though they moved away from the oven, Callie still did not manage to cool down. They sat together on Willow's couch, where Callie was only too aware of their proximity. She cleared her throat. "I liked your motivational poster," she said. Yesterday she'd found a picture of the Leaning Tower of Pisa on her office door. The caption read: "PURPOSE: It's possible that your life is meant to serve as a warning to others."

Hank winked, and then pointed the remote at Willow's TV. "I don't suppose you're a Patriot's fan," he said.

"Can't say that I've ever willingly watched a football game," Callie admitted.

"That's okay." He winced at the screen. "Lately the Pats don't know much about football, either. We'll skip it." He changed the channel. "Hey! Since it's October, there are horror movies on all month long. Check it out—*The Silence of the Lambs*. A classic."

Crap. Callie wasn't good with horror films. On the screen, Jodi Foster wore a frighteningly intense expression. "I'm not brave..." she warned.

Hank only chuckled. "You can hold on to me."

That didn't sound so bad.

Callie put her feet up on Willow's coffee table and watched Hannibal Lecter pace inside his holding cage. She'd forgotten about this part—the creepy escape scene. She lifted her eyes to the kitchen window and noticed that dusk would soon be upon them. The movie soundtrack upped its intensity, and suddenly Callie developed an urge to shut the TV off. "Seriously. I can't watch it. Willow might not have a flashlight."

"For what?" Hank asked, his eyes dancing.

"If it's dark, I'll need it to get back into my car later. To check the backseats."

Hank's mouth split into a big, sexy grin. "But what if he's *under* your car? Watch your ankles."

"Hank!"

He threw his head back and laughed. One of his big hands came out of nowhere and covered hers. Callie closed her eyes and appreciated the warmth of his hand. His thumb came around to stroke her palm.

It was much more fun to concentrate on Hank's touch than on the movie. Now Hannibal's guards were freaking out, and the camera kept cutting to the elevator doors. Callie cringed, knowing what would come next. That dreadful ambulance shot... "Okay, time out!" Callie said, grabbing the remote. She paused the movie and then threw the remote onto one of Willow's chairs.

"You're hysterical."

"Shouldn't we check on the pie, or something?"

Hank scraped a hand over his head. "Sure. In twenty-five minutes or so."

"I'm sorry. But scary movies are not my comfort zone." Callie let out a shaky breath.

When she turned to look at Hank, his eyes were full of humor and warmth. "Wait...you're a *doctor*. But a little gore on the screen...?"

Callie hid her eyes behind one hand. "But there's no creepy music in the E.R."

She expected him to tease her again, but he had other ideas. Hank tugged her arm down, pulling Callie toward him. Startled, her other hand flew out to brace against his body, lest she topple onto his chest. Embarrassingly, she heard herself make an awkward little noise of surprise.

Hank only grinned. "Am I scary, too, Callie?"

"A little," she admitted at a whisper. Because it was true. Even now the intensity of his chocolate gaze made her feel hot and a little out of control.

He ducked his head, brushing his lips against her cheekbone. "But I'm so friendly," he said, his warm breath on her face. Next, those full lips pressed a moist kiss just above her jaw, and Callie began to tingle. His kiss slid sexily down her neck, setting fire to the sensitive skin just beneath her ear. "Kiss me, baby," he rumbled. He raised her chin in one of his big hands, and their mouths finally met. He gave her a couple of soft kisses, his thumbs sweeping her cheekbones. Then, with a sexy growl, his tongue invaded her mouth with a firm sweep.

Oh, yes please.

She wrapped her arms around his hard body and held on for dear life. His kisses were hungry, as if he were starving, and Callie was the last slice of apple tart. As his tongue made eager draws against hers, she felt the nervousness begin to burn right out of her. Rational thought became difficult as his mouth made eager love to her own.

With strong arms, Hank pulled her firmly against his body, his palms singeing her back. Again, his lips burned a trail from the corner of her mouth down her neck. Callie felt herself light up everywhere at once. His confident fingers slid under the hem of her T-shirt, his thumbs raising goose bumps on her stomach. His kisses soldiered on, his lips teasing her collarbone.

Following his lead, Callie's own hands ducked under Hank's shirt. She'd wanted to touch his inked chest since the moment she'd first laid eyes on it. But when her hands grasped his waist, he stiffened, his mouth stalling on her neck.

Whoops! She realized her mistake immediately. Callie had grabbed him right on the transition band—that tricky spot where his injury had wreaked havoc on his nerve endings. Anyone with paralysis had a hypersensitive spot, and she of all people should have known better.

"Sorry," she said quickly, extracting her hands. Backtracking, she raised her hands to his head, skimming her hands over his short hair.

"Mmm," he said approvingly, his arms relaxing around her. His hands slid up the bare skin of her back.

She kissed him again, and all seemed forgiven.

Then, with the slick grace of the well-practiced, Hank unclasped her bra. One hand reached up under the slackened silk, his thumb grazing the swell of her breast. And that was when she began to feel like tinder in a fireplace. His fingers were the matches. A single brush of his thumb across her nipple ignited her. Then both his hands cupped her breasts while his kisses thundered onward. The low moan she heard was of her own making. She was so deep into him then that she could taste more of him than of herself.

Hank eased her down onto the generous sofa. The weight of his hips on hers was tantalizing. How long had it been since she'd been touched? God—a ridiculously long time. Since Nathan. But here she was, flat on her back on Willow's sofa, with the sexiest man she'd ever met splayed on top of her.

He broke off their kiss to slide her T-shirt over her head, and pull her bra away. These were flung on the floor. And then her breasts were in his hands, and he was kissing and licking and sucking their pebbled tips until her hips began to twitch on their own accord.

Willow, guess what I did on your couch? Callie was able to withhold her laugh, but not the giant smile on her face.

"Slide over, gorgeous," Hank said, his voice husky. He wrapped his arms around her and rolled the two of them carefully onto their sides. Callie was trapped against the back of the couch, and she couldn't imagine any better place to be. He hitched himself close, drawing two fingers down from her ear to her jaw. Then he kissed her again, his lips full and wet. She hugged him close to her, the solid wall of muscle that was Hank. The smell of fresh air and apple musk lingered on his clothes.

Hank's free hand slid down her bare torso, through the valley of her breasts and on to her tummy. She shivered as he grazed her navel and headed south toward the waistband of her jeans. "Ohh," she sighed, unashamed of the signal it sent. His hands were very welcome on her body, and there was no point in pretending otherwise.

He listened, fingering the button on her jeans until it gave way, then drawing down the zipper. She gasped as he slid one hand down into her panties, leaving shivers in his wake as he teased the skin below her belly button with his fingertips.

Callie wanted to touch him, too. But how to do that? His shirt was in the way, and she didn't want to try reaching underneath again, even to get at that beautiful chest. She ducked her head, kissing as much of his neck as his tee would allow her to reach.

"We don't need these," he growled, yanking on her jeans.

Callie lifted her hips just in time to feel all the fabric that had covered her falling away. And then she was bare. Hank's hand slid down to cup her between the legs. She took shaky breaths as his tongue stroked hers, and his fingers pressed into exactly the place she wanted them. His thumb grazed her clit and she practically shot upward from the thrill. She hadn't felt this turned on, this out of control in a very long time.

Doctor Callie didn't ever do things like this. Doctor Callie kept the lab coat on and worked double shifts. And look where that had led her? To endless months in an empty bed. To lonely nights critiquing the medical inaccuracies on reruns of *Breaking Bad*.

Hank plunged his tongue into her mouth and his finger

into her willing body. She was on fire, and happy to put herself at his mercy. His fingers circled, and her body wept with joy. She pressed closer to him, wanting more. Wanting *everything*. But Hank was wearing entirely too many clothes. Callie reached down and flipped open the button to his jeans.

Was it her imagination, or did he hesitate then? It was true that they were moving awfully fast. But he'd gotten her naked already. Surely he wasn't going to bail now? She kissed him hard, double checking his enthusiasm. His answer was a sexy groan.

That was all the confirmation she needed. Today she wasn't going to be the nerdy girl who was afraid to make a move. She put her lips against his ear, because even the bravest version of Callie couldn't say what she was about to say above a whisper. "Fuck me, Hank," she breathed. Then, with her fingers on the pull of his zipper, she yanked it down.

And that was when everything stopped.

First, he caught her invading hands in his. Then he let out a long breath. And then he sat up. "No... No. I can't do this."

"What?" she gasped. She was buck naked and sprawled on her friend's couch, panting from lust. And now he was facing away from her, his head in his hands.

"I'm sorry," he said to the air in front of him. "I'm sorry. I didn't mean to end up here."

Callie sputtered, struggling for words. What on earth did he want from her? "How did we end up here if you didn't want to end up here?" Her voice sounded shrill to her own ears.

With his face hidden, for a moment it was absolutely silent. "Old habits die hard," he muttered eventually.

"So..." Her head was spinning. "I wasn't..." She didn't

even have a theory. "You got a look at the goods and decided to put them back on the shelf?"

"That's *not* what just happened." His voice was gruff, and yet he didn't look at her. And it was almost a blessing, because it would be difficult to imagine a more mortifying picture than the one she presented just then. "Callie, I'm sorry."

"Just go," she said, looking around for her clothes. Only her jeans were handy, the panties tangled inside. With shaking hands, she wriggled into them.

His head down, Hank transferred to his chair. He leaned over to shove his feet into his shoes. And then he wheeled toward the door. Callie hunted for her bra while he navigated the old farmhouse door, and the uneven threshold outside. She heard a bump and a curse, but there was no way on earth she would walk over there bare-chested to help him. He probably wouldn't want her to, anyway.

Finally the door slammed shut behind him. Moments later, she heard the engine of his car roar to life.

Callie flopped back on Willow's sofa and let out a giant breath of air. Her heartbeat still felt thready, but she kept it together. She held it all in until the timer beeped several minutes later. The sound of Hank's tires peeling down the driveway had already died. So it was safe to wander over to the oven and open the door. The scent of spiced apples and butter rose into her nostrils. With Willow's oven mitt, she extracted the pan from the oven, setting it on the stove top to cool.

The tart was beautifully browned and bubbling hot. And the sight of it caused a prickle to hatch behind her eyes.

With his hands white-knuckled on the wheel and the gas lever, Hank cranked up the stereo, but even Citizen Cope could not drown out the noise in his head.

He'd been so very stupid.

His mistakes churned in his gut. He should have known better. It was just that he liked her so damn much, and it had made him hope. And hope was an evil bitch. Hope led him down this path, and whispered a lie in his ear.

The lie was simple: that he could still please a woman. And in a sense it was still true. In some alternate universe, there existed a version of events that ended with her creamy thighs spread wide, and his tongue flicking across her clit until she screamed his name. With a little luck, it might have played out like that.

At least for today, anyway.

With Callie, he'd always intended to take things slow. Under no circumstances should he have gotten that amazing girl naked. It was exactly the wrong thing to do. But she was just so goddamned willing, her smooth body reaching for him, opening up to him. If he had only taken it slow, he could still be there with her right now. She might be torturing his mouth with that sweet tongue of hers, and those lips that pursed like a cat's.

But that wasn't what happened, and he'd been a fool to expect her to want him the way he was. She'd asked him for the one thing he couldn't easily give her, and when she'd spoken it—that little three-word request, one he'd welcomed many times in his former life—he'd known the jig was up.

And then, he panicked. Spectacularly. The realization that she was about to put her smooth hands on his useless body… the hopelessness of it all had hit him hard. Because who was he kidding? Eventually it would have all come out.

Or, rather, it *wouldn't* come out, which was the actual problem. Even if he hadn't gone cave man with her on the sofa, it would only have postponed the awkward conversation, and inevitable let down.

No, that would still have been better. If he'd taken it slow, he could have spent more time in her company, pretending that he still had a happy life. And he could have avoided embarrassing her. The intimate words that had sprung from her mouth were still vibrating in the air when he'd abandoned her. She'd been horrified. The look on her face was going to haunt him.

Hank pressed down on the custom hand control and cornered the car around a series of tight curves in the old road. But the memory of her face—the disappointment and the hurt —would not fall away. Hank slowed his speed and was even more honest with himself.

It was a huge mistake to have even kissed her in the first place.

He couldn't be the man she wanted. That guy cracked his back on a half-pipe and disappeared. All that was left was this broken man, who still wanted women but could not hold up his end of the deal in the sack. Where did that leave him? *Alone.* Video games and beer in his decadent bachelor pad. He was thirty-one years old, and all the good times were behind him. And it wasn't only the joys of fucking that he'd miss, but also the possibility of finding someone really special.

He pressed down on the accelerator. Driving fast was often a consolation. But today, even that didn't work. *Shit.* The fucking road was getting blurry. So Hank pulled over, coming to a stop on the shoulder. He rolled down the windows, hoping the October air and the darkening sky would cool him down. Three cows on the other side of the road looked his way, and then went back to chewing their cud.

Hank cut the engine, and then the silence was complete. Even the crickets were done for the year. Aside from his own lonely breathing, the quiet echoed in his ears. He'd better get used to that sound.

The only thing that might take some of the sting away was to go home and crawl inside a bottle of Macallan 18. But even that had its risks. If he ended up in the hospital again, he might manage to embarrass himself to the same woman twice in one day.

Damn.

It was all so fucking wrong, and nothing in the world would ever make it right again.

CHAPTER EIGHT

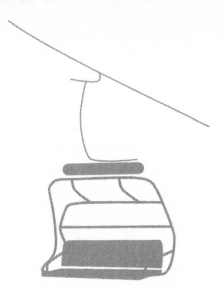

THE NEXT MORNING WAS MONDAY, and Callie had to go to work. But her mortification still hadn't faded. An entire container of Cherry Garcia had not done the trick. She'd lain awake half the night alternately replaying the event and trying to imagine the horror of bumping into him at the hospital this week.

Just to mix it up a little, she also spent an hour or two kicking herself for (almost) hooking up with a study participant. Strictly speaking, they did not have a doctor/patient relationship. Still, there must be a rule against it in some book, somewhere.

When nine o'clock Monday morning inevitably arrived, Callie did what any self-respecting woman would do. She hid from Hank in her office.

Eventually Callie would have to face him. Someday soon, she would have to buck up and offer Hank a smile in the hospital corridor, or a wave in the parking lot. But his rejection was still too raw, too fresh in her mind. So, after checking the therapy schedule like a stalker, she retreated to her desk at 9:40

a.m. Even if he was twenty minutes early for his ten o'clock, they couldn't bump into each other.

She logged in to her computer and got to work entering study data into a spreadsheet. By a few minutes past ten, she began to relax. But then came a knock on the door, and she steeled herself. "Come in."

The door swung open and Hank rolled in.

Damn. It.

He wheeled past the open door and turned to face her desk, his expression unreadable.

Callie stalled, staring down at the clipboard on her desk for a beat. But then she forced herself to meet his eyes, and all the heat she'd felt yesterday threatened to reappear. All too recently she'd had her body wrapped around those big shoulders. Those gorgeous, masculine lips had worshiped her neck and her shoulders. Thank God for the desk acting as a barrier between them. All the things she felt about him were too raw for close proximity.

Hank took a breath that looked pained. "I came to say that I'm sorry I was an ass. I hope we can still be friends."

She had to give him points for bravery. It couldn't have been easy to knock on her office door this morning. But... *Friends.* What woman doesn't dread that word? She could think of literally nothing to say, and there was only a small chance she'd kept the flinch off her face. For the past sixteen hours she'd tortured herself, wondering what she'd done wrong. He'd kissed her like a starving man, and then practically launched himself from the room.

The worst part was that she'd actually said the words "Fuck me, Hank." They had tumbled from her mouth for the first time in her life. She'd let her guard down completely in that moment, and it all went bad. Each time she remembered saying it, she felt like throwing up.

"Callie."

She looked up at him, and an uncomfortable silence settled over the little room. It was her turn to say something, and she found she could not.

A shoe squeaked in the doorway, startling her. Callie swung her chin toward the open doorway, which now framed Nathan.

Damn, damn, damn! How much worse could a morning get, than having *both* of her romantic disasters lurk at her office door?

Oblivious to her discomfort, Nathan cradled a little paper plate in one hand. "Morning, Callie. This apple tart is amazing! Did you make this?"

And now her mortification was complete.

She cleared her throat. "You know damned well I don't bake, Nathan. And I'm kind of busy here..."

He swallowed a bite. "I was hoping you could work a shift for me tomorrow night."

"Tomorrow?" She hesitated. The only positive thing about Nathan's intrusion was that it helped her to stall. She still didn't know what she was going to say to Hank. "Nathan, that's the third time in a week you've asked me to cover for you."

He shrugged. "Your swishy new job leaves us all in the lurch, Callie. Besides, it's a Tuesday night. I'm not asking for New Year's Eve, babe."

Her blood pressure kicked up at notch. The implication was obvious. What did Callie need her evenings free for, anyway? "Why, Nathan?"

"What do you mean, 'why'?"

"Tell me I'm not covering for you so that you can watch *Dancing with the Stars*." She knew all his quirks, and she wasn't afraid to point them out when it suited her.

At this, Hank chuckled, and Nathan turned to look down and around the half open door, spotting him for the first time. "Oh, sorry," Nathan said, forking up another bite of apple tart. "I didn't see you down there."

Nathan's apology could not have sounded more dismissive. Callie cringed again. Lately, she had become very sensitive to the stupid things people often said to wheelchair patients.

This was her life now—a series of embarrassing moments strung between long shifts in a lab coat.

But Nathan went on, oblivious as always. "Since you asked, Shelli and I are going to the Somerset Inn to taste wedding-reception entrées."

Of course they were. And Nathan wouldn't have offered that detail if she hadn't asked for it. *Well played, Callie.* She tried to swallow the lump in her throat.

"Well, will you do it?" he pressed.

Misery made her bold. "Nathan, I'll do your shift if you put the snow tires on my car." They both knew how much she hated going to the dealership. The guys there were slow, and they always treated her like a stupid little woman.

Nathan gave her a look of disbelief. "Are you *kidding* me?"

"Take it or leave it."

He ate the last bite of apple tart. "Fine," he said, chewing. "That's another two hours of my life I'll never get back."

"Nathan, my time is valuable, too."

"But there's overtime pay..." He frowned. "Screw it. You win." He turned around to go. "Can I have another piece of this apple thing?"

"Knock yourself out," she snapped. Finally, he walked away, and Callie dropped her head in defeat. "I'm so sorry about that," she said after a beat.

Hank pushed the door closed. "You just convinced that other doctor to change the tires on your car?"

Callie pressed her forehead into her own hand. "He's not going to do the work himself. His manicure is safe." Nathan's fastidiousness had always bordered on obsessive.

"So the apple tart was good, huh?"

Good was an understatement. Standing alone in Willow's kitchen, she'd eaten a single piece while it was still warm. And it was pure bliss—the crust perfectly flaky, the apples tart and spicy. This morning she'd put the rest of it in the break room, because looking at it made her want to cry. Now, Callie took a deep, slow breath in through her nose. "I can't… Why are you making me talk about this?"

"Callie, I forgot, okay?" His voice was like gravel. "For a few hours, I forgot that I'm a broken asshole. I shouldn't have gone there. I shouldn't have gone anywhere *near* there. I should have said, 'run while you can.'"

The bitterness in his words cut short the endless loop of disappointment running through Callie's head. In the silence between them, she raised her eyes to study his pained face. During her ice cream binge last night, she'd wondered whether he'd run out on her because of performance anxiety. Even though Hank seemed to be hinting at that, she still wasn't sure. She'd already convinced herself that he simply couldn't want someone like her. "Hank," she said quietly, "you aren't *broken*."

His chuckle was dry. "You're right, as usual. Because 'broken' implies the body part in question could be set in a cast and fixed. As things stand…" He cleared his throat again.

"They *don't* stand. I have nothing to offer you or any other woman."

Callie's stomach dropped. In the stacks of research she'd collected about paralysis, a few of the articles were about sex after a spinal cord injury. She hadn't read them yet. But her utter lack of a social life implied that she soon would. "Hank, you... I'd bet good money that...things aren't as bad as you're making them sound. Maybe you're being a bit overanxious."

He glowered at her. "I'm being *realistic.* I can't be your guy or anyone else's. Small wonder that I sometimes end up at the wrong end of a tequila bottle."

The look on his face was so guarded, so vulnerable, that she would have to choose her words carefully. Those dark brown eyes would not quite meet hers.

"Hank, listen to me. I'm saying this as your friend, and as a semi-knowledgeable medical professional. You need to visit a urologist, for your own future sanity. Because some day you'll meet someone who will make you wish you had."

"Meet someone? But you... I..." He rubbed his temples as if he had terrible pain there. "There's no point. Why run the race if you can't cross the finish line?"

She felt her mouth fall open. Could this really be how men thought about sex? "Because it's not a *race,* Hank." And now everything was just a hopeless mess. Hank had just revealed to her that he was troubled by a medical issue. Yet because of their debacle on Willow's sofa, she was now exactly the wrong person to advise him.

Callie grabbed the hospital directory off her desk, flipped it upon to the urology department and thrust it toward him. "Look, if you want, we'll never mention yesterday again. But for your own sake, call these guys. They're going to tell you that anyone with a spinal cord injury can have a fulfilling romantic life. It just might look a little different than your old one."

"Jesus." Hank snatched the booklet from her hand and then threw it back down on her desk. "Callie, you're not listening. And do you hear yourself? There are an infinite number of variations of the 'adjust your expectations' speech, aren't there?" His face flushed, and his eyes flashed. "I'm so tired of people trying to sell me on my new shitty life, telling me how great it really is. It's my damned life, and I can hate it if I want to."

Callie felt an unwelcome prickle behind her eyes. "Then go ahead! There's the door."

His face fell. "I did not come in here to yell at you. I came to apologize for putting you in an awkward position."

She felt her throat closing up. "Got it. Now you're twenty minutes late for your session."

Aiming a final, sad look at her, he opened her office door and rolled out.

On a scale where zero was a poor result, and ten was perfection, Callie's mood for the next ten days equated to approximately negative three thousand.

When Callie wasn't at the hospital, she filled her free time with bad television, ice cream and medical articles. She was surprised to find that very little useful research had been done on sex after spinal-cord injuries. On those pages where the scholarly journals did bother to cover the topic, the focus was mainly on fertility. And what little information she found suggested that patients had sexual outcomes that varied as widely as their injuries. While some stories were sad, there were complete quadriplegics who had fathered babies the old-fashioned way.

The most depressing result of all Callie's stewing was realizing that there was no ethical way to help Hank. The man needed an intervention. But getting naked with him meant she was the only one on the hospital staff who couldn't offer advice.

What a mess she'd made. And now they were avoiding each other in the hospital corridors, like a couple of angst-filled teenagers.

It was all so very sad. The pain in Hank's brown eyes weighed on her. She couldn't help but remember the first time she'd seen him. *Sex on a snowboard*, she'd thought then. Now he was at war with himself. And there didn't seem to be a single thing she could do about it.

It made her wonder—which was worse? To have felt sexy and lost it, or to never have felt sexy at all?

CHAPTER
NINE

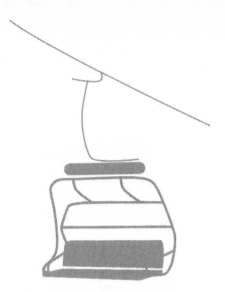

ON A FRIDAY AFTERNOON IN MID-OCTOBER, Hank did a session on the FES bike, followed by an hour with Tiny in the PT room. That misnamed giant worked him like a draft horse—yoking him into a harness over the parallel bars, and forcing him to swing his lower body along in a strange parody of walking. Before the session ended, his arms and shoulders were shaking.

"That's it, man," Tiny would say each time Hank gained a foot down the mat.

But Hank wasn't exactly hearing the theme song to *Rocky* in his head anymore. He knew he was supposed to be enthusiastic about standing upright and moving his body. But his progress had plateaued. Physical therapy was his full-time job. And all he had to show for his trouble was a spastic eight feet of movement, all while he was supported like an I-beam from a crane.

Afterward, Hank wheeled his exhausted body into the men's locker room. There, he heard male voices behind the door to the pool. It was after six, and the day's sessions were finished. There was laughter, and he found himself wheeling over to find its source. He pushed the door open, and the laughter died as three faces looked up at him from the large hot tub in the corner.

"At ease, boys. It's not the authorities," said one of the three men, who had once introduced himself as Big Mike. "Get in here, Lazarus. And close the door."

Hank wheeled across the pool deck toward them. "Is this where the party is?" Since he usually left the hospital after his sessions ended, he didn't know these guys very well. He was pretty sure they were all Iraq vets.

"We hang out here some on Fridays," another dude said. Hank was pretty sure his name was Dave. "Hop in already."

Hank looked down at his track pants. "Sounds like fun, but I don't have a suit. Didn't have an aqua session today." And even if he did have a suit, it would take a year to change into it. He was just so tired of the extra effort everything required.

Big Mike shrugged. "I didn't bother with a suit. We won't look at your hairy ass. Promise."

"I'll move over," Dave added, shifting himself down the bench to make room. "Because I love playing footsie with Evan."

"Go ahead," the third guy said. "It's not like I can feel it." The joke earned him a laugh from his pals and a high five from Big Mike.

Hank listened to the soothing bubble and splash of the jets, and felt the steam calling to him. And in his old life, he'd skinny-dipped his way across every ski resort in the western United States. Getting naked was never something he'd had trouble with. What had changed?

Just everything.

"All right. Fuck it," he heard himself say.

The third guy—Evan—reached for a towel he'd stashed behind his head and hurled it at Hank. "Thanks, man," Hank said, draping it over his lap while he shimmied out of his drawers. With the towel covering the important stuff, he transferred to the side of the tub, then hoisted each leg in turn into the hot water. The last thing he did was to press up, easing his body into the churning warmth. "Hell yes," he sighed as the heat enveloped him.

"That's right," Big Mike said. "That's why we sneak in here before happy hour. Don't turn us in."

Hank tipped his head back and sighed. "I'm not much of a rule follower myself."

"You don't look like one," someone chuckled.

"So I gotta ask," Big Mike said, and Hank had no idea what question was about to hit him. "Which hand controls did you put on that Panamera Turbo?"

Oh. That was an easy one. "We went with the Menox. And I'm really happy with it."

"That's a sweet ride, man."

Hank grinned. "I always drove a beat-up old 4Runner. But my parents bought me that thing after...you know." He cleared his throat. "After my sudden midlife crisis."

Big Mike's eyes went wide. "Damn. It's almost worth it."

Hank laughed for the first time in days. "If you say so, dude."

Then Big Mike began discussing the merits and flaws of the different hand-control systems, and Hank felt some of the past week's tension leave his body. He wasn't really in the market for new friends, but sitting here was a lot less depressing than heading home to his empty house, and eating a reheated meal in front of the TV.

He cupped some of the hot water over his sweaty neck and let the conversation swirl around him, just as the water did.

They're telling me I should think about getting the pump," Dave said.

"Aw, Christ," his buddy said.

There was a small silence, and Hank broke it by asking, "What's a pump?"

Big Mike pointed at Hank. "If you don't know, you're damned lucky."

Lucky. There was that word again. But coming from these guys it didn't sound so bad.

"It's a device inserted under the skin," Dave said, rolling his neck. "It's supposed to stop spasms."

Big Mike just shook his head. "My legs would have to be doing the Macarena all night long for me to get that thing. Kowalsky got the pump, and now he can't get it up anymore."

"That's what he told me," Dave said, his face glum. "But when Jenny and I get it on, half the time I get too jiggy to finish."

"But at least you still have the other half of the time," his friend pointed out. "If you get the pump, you might not even have that."

Hank swept a palm-full of water across his face to hide his surprise. He tried to remember if he'd *ever* heard a guy admit to having a problem with sex before. "What we really need right now is some beer," he said.

"Then let's move this party," Big Mike agreed. "Skunk Hollow?"

"How about Rupert's?" Hank countered.

"That place is kind of pricey," someone said.

That made Hank feel like an ass, because the guy was right. In Hamilton, near the ski hill, they charged tourist prices.

Money was the only problem Hank didn't really have. "I've been meaning to see if it's true that my little sister is working there. So how about I buy a couple of rounds?" Then he heard himself add something else to the equation. "Just as long as you'll all give me the name of your favorite urologist."

"Deal!" a couple of them yelled at once.

"Ha!" Big Mike laughed. "Does this mean you haven't met Doctor Dick?"

"Can't say that I've had the pleasure." Hank edged down into the pool a little farther, beginning to regret bringing it up.

"He's a weird old hippie who gets off on the fact that he gets paid to talk about dicks all day."

"There are probably worse jobs," Hank pointed out.

"True," Big Mike agreed. "We'll give you his number, on one condition."

"What?"

"You have to promise to go."

Hank shrugged. "Sure."

"You say that now," Big Mike said, adjusting the towel behind his head. "But nobody wants to look a doctor in the eye and say out loud that his trouser snake won't stand up when he wants it to. They try to make it easier for us. There's a form to fill out in the waiting room. But it still sucks. Nobody our age wants to check the box next to 'erectile dysfunction.'"

There was an awkward silence until Evan said, "You're really selling this, dude."

That made everyone chuckle, although Hank felt the laughter stick in his chest.

"He's right, though," Mike said. "It has to be done. We *all* take vitamin V. It's the best thing ever invented."

Even though Hank suspected that some real wisdom had just been tossed his way, the knot in his chest made it difficult to appreciate. "Can we go drink a whole lot of beer now?" he asked.

"Absofuckinglutely," Big Dave agreed.

Callie eased her car into a parking spot on Main Street just as her phone began to ring. She knew before she even looked that it was Willow calling again. Callie had been ducking her friend, because she wasn't ready to share what had gone down between herself and Hank. Though, if she and Willow were sitting together somewhere, a bottle of wine between them, the story would have easily slipped out.

Callie missed Willow terribly. And phone calls just weren't the same thing.

She answered her phone, because if she didn't, Willow was going to start to worry. "Hello?"

"Callie! Thank you so much."

"What did I do?"

"The house! We accepted an offer! After all this time, that sucker is finally going to sell."

"That's *great*, sweetie. I'm so happy for you. But I don't think I had a thing to do with it."

"It gets better!" Willow chirped. "This means I get to see you. The closing should happen next month. Please tell me you're not on the verge of some long vacation. Because I'm not coming to Vermont if you're not there."

Callie smiled into her phone. "No worries. Where would I go? Except..."

"Except what?"

Callie wrestled with the thought of telling Willow her latest idea. If she said it out loud, then it went from an idea to a plan.

"There's a job in California," she blurted. "I'm thinking of applying for it."

Willow was silent for a moment. "Gosh, Callie. What brought that on? Are your parents okay?"

"They're fine," she said quickly. "But I need a change." Callie opened her car door and climbed out, shoving her keys into her purse.

"Wow. Where's the job?"

Fifteen minutes later, Callie leaned her elbows on the polished wood of the bar, while her friend Travis Rupert tapped her a beer. "How's work?" he asked, setting down a coaster for her.

"Work is great," she said, taking the glass from him. "But work is never the problem, is it?"

Travis opened both his arms wide, taking in the attractive interior of his business. "Nope. Work is great. It's the rest of my life that leaves a little to be desired." Travis was another member of the lonely hearts club. He'd been half in love with Willow last year. But she'd picked Dane instead.

"This is your busy season, right?" Callie asked.

"One of them. There's a lull after foliage season. That's when I start praying for snow. The more it snows, the more thirsty skiers I'll get." He wiped down the bar. "So. Did Doctor Jerkface get dumped yet?" Travis had a theory that karma would bite Callie's ex in the ass. But every passing month his prediction seemed a little more ridiculous.

"Nope!" Callie said cheerfully. "But I don't have to watch him fondle her backside in the break room anymore, because now I have an office to hide in."

"You're moving up in the world, Callie."

She smiled at him over the rim of her pint glass. Unfortunately, she was starting to feel as if her job was holding the rest of her life back. Sure, it had made sense to put career first for these past few years. She had student loans to repay, and that was scary. But her personal life had suffered. If she took that job in California, it would mean giving up her comfy little research project here. But a year from now the study would end, anyway. And the little Vermont hospital wouldn't likely have another one like it.

And then where would Callie be? Here. Alone. And working the same job she'd had before. Eventually, Nathan and his nurse would ask her to cover a shift so that they could go to obstetrical appoints to coo over the sonogram images of their future offspring.

Ugh! Callie needed to shake up her life before it came to that.

She was distracted from this grumpy reverie by a whispered curse behind her. Callie turned to see Stella Lazarus with a jar of cherries in one hand and a tipping tray in the other. From the tray, limes rolled and dove onto the floor. Reaching out, Callie relieved Stella of the jar of cherries. Setting it on the bar, she slid off the stool to help the younger woman retrieve the limes which were scattering across the floor like so many marbles.

"Thanks," Stella huffed, gathering limes in her apron.

"No problem," Callie said, catching one that had rolled under her bar stool. When she'd walked in earlier, Callie had been more than a little surprised to learn who Travis's new employee was. She had no idea why Stella would go from foundation work to wiping down tables. There was probably a story there, but Callie didn't know Stella well enough to ask.

It was obvious, though, that Stella didn't seem have a lot of waitressing experience. This was the second little disaster that Callie had witnessed inside of half an hour. As she'd taken her seat at the bar, Stella had greeted her and then immediately dropped a martini glass on the floor.

"Heads up." Travis tossed Stella a basket for the fruit, and to catch it, Stella almost lost control of the limes in her apron.

"Ack," Stella sighed, setting the full basket on the bar. Ducking under the pass-through, she joined Travis in back.

"Now wash them," Travis prompted her. "Those are going to end up in the drinks."

"If I don't spill the drinks first," Stella grumbled. She brought the basket over to the sink and began rinsing the fruit.

"You're a good girl, Stella," Travis said. "Hang in there."

She shut off the water, and laughed her smoky laugh. "I'd rather be a good waitress than a good girl, Trav."

Callie wondered if she and Travis merely enjoyed flirting, or if maybe they were seeing each other. She was probably too young for him, although Callie hoped the bartender would find somebody. In a small town like Hamilton, Vermont, it was awfully hard to find your mate.

At least, that was what Callie needed to tell herself. Because if the population of Windsor County wasn't really at fault, than what was? If Callie's loneliness was her own fault, then moving several thousand miles across the country wouldn't help.

But that couldn't be true. There had to be an awful lot of single men in California. Hot, single men who were eager to hook up with nerdy female doctors.

Callie took a deep pull of her beer and thanked her lucky stars that for once she was not on call. As she set the glass down on the bar, a cool breeze brushed her cheek. The outside door had opened, and she instinctively turned toward the vestibule to see if perchance a handsome stranger had walked in. Hope springs eternal.

"Hey, it's Doctor C!" Big Mike called out as he rolled into the room. He was followed by Dave.

"Hi guys!" She waved. She'd never run into her study participants at Rupert's before, but seeing them here shouldn't surprise her. There weren't very many bars in a fifty-mile radius.

Big Mike and Dave headed for the large table near the window. Stella jumped off her bar stool. "I'll just get those chairs out of the way," she said.

"Much obliged," Big Mike said with a wink. "There are going to be four wheelchairs here. We're having a convention, see. And we're definitely buying that girl a drink." He made his hand into a gun and fired it at Callie.

"Roger that," Stella said, stacking four chairs together. Then she picked up the stack and carried them out of the room.

Big Mike and Dave rolled up to the table, and Callie wondered which other two were about to roll in. As if on cue, Hank's face appeared in the doorway.

And then two things happened in quick succession. First, her heart tripped over itself. Because Hank still had that effect on her. But that sensation was immediately followed by utter discomfort. *Crap.* He gave her a chin lift, and she returned it with a weak smile.

That was the trouble with small towns. When your naked exploits ended badly, there was nowhere to hide. "I have to get out of Vermont," Callie breathed.

"Is it that bad, sweetheart?" Travis asked. "Are you in trouble with the law?" His green eyes twinkled.

She shook her head. *Keep it together, Callie.* "I'm fine. Never mind." Travis knew all about her issues with Nathan, but she hadn't told him—or anyone else—how she felt about Hank. It hurt too much to be bar-stool chatter.

"Are you really thinking about leaving?"

Even though she could hear the sexy rumble of Hank's voice talking to the other guys, she raised a finger to her lips. Travis came closer. "I can't really talk about it. But there's a job posted in Marin County. If they hired me, I'd be ninety minutes from my parents, and a very short flight away from Willow and Dane."

Travis smiled. "How is she doing, anyway? Have you heard from her?"

"I haven't seen her since the Olympics, but she sent me some pictures. The baby had her first birthday last month. Hang on…" Callie hopped off her barstool and fetched her purse off the kick ledge beneath it. She scrolled through the inbox on her phone for the photos.

As she stood there, Hank startled her by rolling up beside her. As his handsome face came into her line of sight, Callie's throat got tight.

"Hazardous!" Travis boomed out. "How've you been?"

"Great," Hank said, but the expression on his face disagreed. He looked uncomfortable, and so Callie looked away. He slid a credit card onto the bar. "Can you make sure I'm covering that table?" He cocked his chin toward the guys from the therapy program.

"Easily done," Travis said, picking up the card. "Hey, Callie, Hank—you two know each other?"

"Sure," Callie said quickly, at the same time Hank said "Yeah."

There was an awkward pause while Travis turned to prop Hank's credit card up on the cash register. Then he turned back to look at the photos. "Aw, I never thought I'd see this." Travis laughed as he scrolled over to a cute picture of Dane asleep on a sofa, with Finley passed out on his chest. "The fact that someone calls Dane 'Daddy' scares the crap out of me." He set the phone down and moved down the bar to take another customer's order.

Hank plucked the phone off the bar and considered it. "That's a regular Hallmark card right there," he said. His face closed up, becoming totally unreadable. He put the phone down. Without another word, he went back to his friends.

Callie watched him retreat, and was nudged by her very first memory of Hank. He'd given Dane a terrible hard time, hadn't he? He'd called Dane "whipped," and scoffed at the idea that family obligation might trump a night out partying.

Don't forget that, Callie ordered herself. Maybe she and Hank were doomed even before their naked mishap. Even though he could still make her heart speed up just by entering the room, Callie wanted a family someday. But nothing about Hank said "family man." And even if they'd managed to have wild monkey sex together, that would still be true.

Right. *California.* That was the new plan.

But even with her back to him, it was as if Callie could feel Hank's pull. When something funny was said at their table, she heard his husky laugh, and it tugged at her.

Though Callie had decided that Hank was a lost cause, her heart hadn't gotten the memo.

"What's up with that?" Travis whispered, wiping down the bar just in front of her.

Callie tried for a noncommittal shrug. She'd forgotten that Travis had a bartender's sixth sense for reading every situation. "I know him from the hospital. He's part of the therapy clinic that I'm working on."

"Interesting." Travis filled a cocktail shaker with ice. "And now you want to move a few thousand miles away?"

"Let it go, Trav," Callie begged.

"I will. But only because his sister is coming back."

Callie looked up to see Stella emerging from the kitchen with a tray of lit candles, one for each table. She made her way over to the wheelchair crew, sliding a basket of pretzels down in front of them. Then she cocked the tray onto her hip and deadpanned: "Coffee, tea or me?"

There was a moment of surprised silence, while Callie watched Hank's lips twitch with amusement. "Boys, don't answer that. This is my kid sister, Stella. She and I used to be tight, until she lost my phone number."

"Hank," she murmured. "I did not lose your phone number. I've been busy."

He grabbed her by the hips and pulled her onto his knee. "Busy? Mom says you're working here six nights a week now just to piss her off."

"*Challenge*," Stella said with a roll of her eyes. "Our mother has never said 'piss' in her life."

"I was paraphrasing. But what gives? You aren't exactly the waitress type."

"Says who?" Stella argued. "I'm going to be a good waitress."

"Really? Then how come I don't have a beer in front of me?"

Stella stood up and folded her arms. "What would you have to drink, sire?"

"What do you have on tap, wench?"

"Well..." Stella took a step toward the bar and squinted at the tap handles.

Behind the bar, Travis just shook his head. "I'm going to tattoo the beer list on your hand, Stella."

"You might as well tattoo it on my boobs. Because that's where the customers are usually looking, anyway."

"Yeah, and I really don't need to know that," Hank muttered.

Travis began to rattle off the tap beers. "Switchback Ale, Guinness, U.F.O., Long Trail and Woodchuck Cider."

"Long Trail," Hank said. After the other guys ordered, Stella went to move away. But Hank caught her hand. "We're not done, baby sister. Tell me why you're working in a bar."

"I need money to go to Alaska. Mom retracted her offer to pay. So I got a job. It's not a very complicated story." Her eyes flared, daring her brother to argue.

Hank cocked his head. "You had a job. At the foundation. You were going to work on that wildlife survey project—who's going to finish that now?"

"Not my problem," she answered, a hand on her hip.

"The wildlife survey is important."

"Hank, the environment is your thing. Not mine. And giving away money is Mom's thing. And building ski resorts is Dad's thing."

"And this—" Hank gestured around the room "—is your thing."

Travis snorted into the cash register.

"I'm just asking," Hank tried, "whether ditching the foundation is your best move?"

She crossed her arms. "I think it's my only move. I'm not going to change my life's goals because Mommy and Daddy don't like them."

"They're just..." Hank sighed.

"...Scared," she finished. "One kid almost killed himself,

and they don't want to go through that again. So the other one gets chained into her room. At twenty-six years old."

Hank looked her over. "I don't see any shackles."

"The desk inside Dad's empire—that's my shackle. I'm supposed to sit at it until I start popping out babies."

There was a silence, and Callie played with her beer coaster, feeling guilty to find the Lazarus family drama so fascinating.

"Stella...maybe we shouldn't do this here," Hank prompted, his voice all honey and smoke.

"It was your idea, big brother. You brought it up. And now you know what I'm up against. I'd rather sling beer than do it their way. Now, if you'll excuse me." She tucked her tray against her side and went back toward the kitchen again.

"Your little sister is a spitfire," Big Mike said when she was out of earshot.

"That she is," Hank agreed. "We can only hope that she'll get over her snit long enough to bring us those beers."

"I've got you covered," Travis called. "Another beer, Callie?"

"Yes sir. Because somehow this first one disappeared."

"Happens to the best of us, Callie. Can I order you something to eat, maybe a BLT?"

"That would be great." Travis wasn't trying to upsell her. It's just that he knew that two beers was one more than she usually drank. Living in a tiny town, where everyone knew your quirks and disasters, used to be appealing. But when you were lonely, it didn't feel like such a great bargain.

"Stella," Travis called. "Can you bring Callie a BLT on wheat toast, with the tomato and mayo on the side? And two pickles." He knew her order perfectly.

Yup. Time to move on.

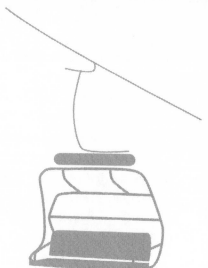

CHAPTER
TEN

"GIVE IT SOME MORE GAS," Tiny coached. "More! That's how we do it down in Georgia!"

Hank had had just about all that he could take today, and the trainer's motor mouth wasn't helping. His muscles were shaking, and his body would not do as he asked.

"Tighten those abs. You can make it all the way to the wall," Tiny urged him on.

But Hank could not, in fact, get anywhere near the damn wall. Instead of explaining this in a calm voice, he screamed an obscenity at the top of his lungs.

That's when the therapy-room door opened, and Callie's startled face appeared in the opening. "Everything okay in here, guys?" The words were casual, but a quaver in her voice betrayed her discomfort.

Perfect. Just fucking perfect.

Hank thought he'd already found all the ways he could look like an ass in front of Callie. Who knew he could manage to find one more? It wasn't Tiny's fault that Hank couldn't walk. And there was really no excuse for losing it during a therapy session.

"We're just fine, Callie." Tiny's voice was meant to sound soothing.

Callie stood there a moment longer, and Hank wished he could sink into the floor. He hadn't seen her for a few days, and he hated that she was seeing him like this—face red, T-shirt drenched. He was wearing braces that came up all the way to his hips, and leaning hard on the ugliest granny walker he'd ever seen.

"Let's go," Tiny said in a calm voice, pointing toward the wall.

But Hank only shook his head. Time slowed to a crawl, the tense silence threatening to swallow them all whole. Hank stared down at his sneakers and wished he could be anyplace else.

Eventually, he heard the sound of Callie ducking out of the room again, and closing the door behind her.

Without a word, Tiny pulled Hank's chair up behind him. Hank sat down, and bent to unlock the knees of his braces.

"Don't touch those, dude. You're not done."

"I am fucking done."

"Nope. I got one more thing planned." He swiveled Hank around, positioning him in front of the heavy bag hanging from the ceiling. Plucking the gloves off the floor, he handed them to Hank. "Up you go. Come on." Wordlessly, Hank shoved his hands into the gloves. Tiny locked the legs of Hank's braces, and then pulled him up. He kicked the wheelchair away. Then he stood behind Hank, steadying him with two hands on Hank's rib cage. "Kill it, man."

Hank took a deep breath. Then he drew back one of his powerful arms and nailed the bag.

"Harder," Tiny insisted.

Hank drilled the bag, and it was exhausting. But somehow it was exactly what he needed. If anything, he put more into each successive punch than he'd put into the last.

"That's it, man. Get it out."

Hank squared his shoulders and lit into the bag again. Then he opened his mouth and roared. The sound was full of fury and pain.

Then he adjusted his glove and hauled off to hit the bag again.

The next day, Callie looked up to find Tiny's great girth blocking her office door. "Hey, girlfriend! Got a minute?"

"For you? Always."

Tiny crossed his arms over his massive chest and cocked his head. "Dr. Callie, can you do Hank a favor?"

"What?"

"If you want Hank's therapy observed, send someone else."

"Okay. Why?"

Tiny scratched his chin. "He doesn't like you to watch. Whenever you put your head in, everything grinds to a halt. I think it's because you're a pretty lady, and he doesn't want to struggle in front of you."

"I just put my head in to find out why he was shouting at you. Because that shouldn't be part of a therapy session."

His face was thoughtful. "That's usually true. But Hank is trying to work through some anger right now. And the gym can sometimes be a safe place to do that. So lately...that's how it is between us. I take his bullshit, and then I say, 'for that, I want ten more reps.' And he always shuts up and gives it to me."

"I think I understand. But are we missing something here?" Callie stretched a hand up to her own aching shoulder. "Should someone be even more worried for him, then?"

"Not necessarily. Hank is coming up on the one-year anniversary of his injury. Next month, actually. And that's kind of a big deal." Tiny stepped behind Callie, putting his own hands on her shoulder. "Uh oh, boss. You got quite the knot here."

He sank his thumbs into her muscle, and Callie might have fainted with relief. "Wow," she whispered while his hands showed her shoulder who's boss.

"Yeah, it's a bad one. Lean forward and drop your head."

She slumped onto her desk, and his magic hands continued to coax the stress from her shoulders. "Are you saying that Hank thinks he'll never improve? Because it's been a year?"

"That's probably his fear. There's nothing magic about the one-year mark. But look at his life—he does rehab like it's his full-time job. Every day, almost. He isn't walking, and he's starting to realize that it isn't going to happen for him."

"So…" Callie felt the truth of it in the pit of her stomach. "He's *failed*. At his full-time job." It was her own very worst fear.

"Yeah. And I bet he has no idea what to do about that."

Chastened, Callie took a very deep breath. She'd been nursing her own disappointment over how things turned out with Hank. But it was nothing like the disappointment he was working through. In that moment, it all became so much easier to bear. He'd said, *I hope we can be friends.* And she'd chafed at the sound of it. But she cared about him, and that was all that mattered. If he needed a friend, that was what she'd be. It was a simple as that.

Behind her, Tiny continued to work his skillful thumbs into her neck muscles, and the friction of his fingers on her skin felt soul-healing. *This is exactly what I need,* she thought.

But what did Hank need?

In the first place, the tension between them needed to end. She could manage that now. What Hank needed from her was the only thing that she could give him: compassion and forgiveness. And empathy. It was brutally simple, but also true.

She actually felt the moment when the knot in her shoulder relaxed.

"*There* it is," Tiny said, satisfaction in his voice.

"Tiny? Now would be a really good time to ask me for a raise."

He giggled. "Can I have a raise?"

"Unfortunately, no. But if it were up to me..." She let her head fall forward another inch. "You have no idea how much better you just made my day."

"Then maybe it is a good time for me to ask you a favor. I chipped a tooth. And the dentist can fit me in tomorrow at four-thirty. Otherwise, I have to wait three days."

"Four-thirty..." Callie tried to think, but her mind was turning to a happy mush as Tiny worked his fingers up to the base of her skull.

"I'm with Hank at that hour. But I'd have to leave halfway through our session. I don't know what that does to your data, but I was thinking he wouldn't mind cutting it short."

"Okay, Tiny. That's fine. Maybe I'll find someone else to take over for you. Leave it to me."

When Hank rolled into the locker room the next afternoon, he found another parody of an inspirational poster stuck to his locker door. This one was a picture of a meadow full of daisies. The caption was: "BLOOM WHERE YOU'RE PLANTED. Because that's what plants do. And I've never heard one complaining."

Hank chuckled to himself. Maybe Callie had decided that she wanted to be buddies again. And that was a good thing, even if glimpses of her gave him an ache in his gut.

In the therapy room, Hank noticed that Tiny was taking it easy on him today. The dreaded walker had been stashed in a corner, and the weight bench took center stage. "I thought we'd do some chest and back," the big trainer said. "I don't want you blaming me if your bench press suffers."

"Uh huh. Listen, Tiny. If we work on walking today, I swear I won't lose it."

"I know you won't. But I have to leave in fifteen minutes, and I don't know if Doctor C. found someone to replace me."

"Nobody could replace you, big guy," Hank drawled.

"Aw, now you're laying it on a little thick. Do you want to press, or should we fool around with some pull-ups?"

Hank gave his shoulders a circle or two and eyed Tiny. "Do you do pull-ups, big man?"

The trainer grinned. "I've been known to chin that bar a few times. Why?"

"How about a little wager? The longest series wins."

Tiny crossed his arms and chuckled. "What do I win when I best you?"

"Let's keep it simple, because I don't want to hurt you too

bad. Subtract the loser's reps from the winner's, and the difference is the number of beers he owes the winner."

"Fine. But you go first."

Hank rolled over to the bar, realizing that he had no clue how he was going to get up on it. But Tiny walked over and knelt down in front of him. "Come on. Piggyback."

Huh. Hank tipped forward and wrapped his arms around Tiny's neck. The trainer rose into the air, catching Hank's bent knees and rising to a standing position. A second later, Hank was eye level with the bar. He grabbed it, and Tiny stepped away again.

Not wasting any time, Hank adjusted his grip and pulled. "One," he said, lowering himself.

"Two," Tiny counted for him. "Three." The big man used the toe of his sneaker to kick the big crash mat underneath Hank. "Four. Five. Six…"

Hank tried to set a pace that he could sustain. He hadn't done pull-ups in a long time. But he did plenty of curls, and used his upper body all day long. It felt good to heave his carcass into the air just like any chump.

"Twelve. Thirteen. I may be in trouble," Tiny chuckled.

"Hi guys! What's happening?"

At the sound of Callie's voice, Hank clenched his jaw. Now he had to win this thing. It was a matter of dignity.

"Sixteen… oh, he's slowing down! Hallelujah. Seventeen… Eighteen. Shit."

Hank's arms were shaking like crazy. He was going to pay for this tomorrow, but it would probably be worth it. The bar was slicked with his sweat now. So this would be over soon.

"Nineteen… Twenty. That's plenty, right? Twenty-one…"

That was all he could take. Hank let go, reaching for the

mat with his forearms. He landed with a bounce and a laugh. "Batter up!"

"What are you hooligans up to, anyway? Don't you have to leave?" Callie asked Tiny.

"I'm not leaving until I win this thing. Just a friendly little contest. Move that ass, Hank."

He rolled to the edge of the mat and sat up. Tiny locked his chair in front of him, so Hank pressed down on the armrests and hauled himself up. His arms were like jelly.

"Good thing you don't need your arms to count. Unless you count on your fingers?" Tiny kicked the mat out of the way and wiped down the bar.

"Can I leave my shoes on?" Hank asked. "If you're only going to do ten, I won't need to count my toes."

"Smart…" Tiny said, gripping the bar for his first pull-up. "Ass…" he let out on the second one.

Hank watched as the trainer did eight pull-ups in a row, very fast. He cleared his throat and then did his best imitation of Tiny. "Aw, that's looking good, man! Real good! I knew you could hang with the big kids."

Tiny gave a half laugh and tried to ignore him.

"Work it, baby," Hank said on the tenth rep. "They want to see it in the back row."

Callie began to giggle. "Jeez, Hank. You sound just like him."

"Don't slow down yet, man!" Hank kept up the commentary. "Give it some more gas. Yeah! That's how we do it in Georgia."

Callie howled, and Tiny gave a frustrated snort. His arms shook on the fifteenth rep. Slowly, he did three more, and then hung there a second. That pause—that was the death of pull-ups. As Hank watched, Tiny pulled one more time. And then failed to clear the bar. "Damn," he said, putting his feet down, dropping his hands in defeat. "Rematch next week?"

"Hell yes," Hank agreed. "But I'll be practicing."

When the trainer walked out, Callie turned to him. "You do a mean impression of Tiny," she said, her smile genuine. It tugged at his heart to see it.

"I'm just here to amuse."

"He had to go to the dentist. I didn't get anybody to fill in, because I thought you could use a break from playing Simon Says with the training staff."

Hank hesitated. She had his number. She always did. And what's more, he couldn't stop noticing the V her blouse made, or the way the buttons strained gently across her bust. *Quit looking, asshole. You don't get to see that again.* He dragged his face up to her eyes. "I may have lost my cool yesterday. But it's all right. I'm good now."

"Still," she said, licking her lips. The sight of it made him want to kiss her. "Everybody needs a day off."

"So…" He hesitated. "I should just go home early?"

"You could," she said. "But I had a better idea."

He waited for her to say what it was, hoping his face wouldn't flush and betray the naughty place those words made his mind go.

She smiled at him. "Yesterday Tiny gave me the most amazing shoulder massage, and it changed my life."

Hank couldn't help but chuckle. He dropped his eyes, though, because it hurt too much to look at her pretty face. He couldn't name another woman who had ever gotten so far under his skin.

"I thought I'd pay it forward. If you'll let me."

He probably did a poor job of keeping the surprise off his face. "Why?"

She shrugged, her cheeks pinking up. "You wanted us to be friends. I'm being friendly. Lie down on the table, would you? And take your shirt off."

Damn. Even though he'd hurt her, here she stood, trying to make things better between them. She was so strong, and Hank felt like a heel. He wanted to say no, because he found it excruciating to be so close to her. But that would only offend her more.

She sighed. "Or you can just go home early instead. But do you get regular massages?"

"No." He shifted in his chair. "I've thought about it. But I'd need to find someone who knows not to handle my transition area. It's uncomfortable." Callie would know what he meant.

She frowned. "I understand. But I think you would really benefit from massage. If you're not comfortable with me touching your back, I can call around and try to find someone else with SCI experience."

He grabbed his T-shirt with both hands and lifted. "We'll give it a try."

"You don't sound sure," she pressed. "If you'd rather go home, or go soak in the whirlpool, that's all good, too."

He pressed his hands onto the table and transferred with a twist of his hips. "Well…" He attempted a laugh. "You're not going to punish me, are you? Not that I don't have it coming."

"I guess you'll find out," she said, her lips twitching. "Why don't you just take it like a man." She pointed to the end of the table. "Lie down. Let's see how tight you really are."

How tight? Plenty. He maneuvered into position, lying on his stomach and bringing his arms up over his head. He used to get massages all the time, before his accident. There was a place in Park City he particularly enjoyed. The girl's name was

Hella. Once she'd figured out that he was an excellent tipper, the massages got even better.

It hadn't even seemed like a big deal back then. Just another cheap thrill in his hedonistic life. But now the memory only made him feel hollow.

Callie began by placing her smooth hands on his neck, working her fingers into his muscles. He closed his eyes, trying to think of nothing else. Although, maybe she was waiting for him to apologize one more time. "Callie…"

"Hush, okay?" she interrupted. "Unless you want to tell me something about what I'm doing right here, it can wait. Just relax."

Fuck it. Her hands were strong, and his neck was tight. He sighed, allowing his body to melt onto the table. She rolled her thumbs in small circles on the back of his skull. "Shit, yes," he said.

"There you go," she murmured.

He floated under the pressure of her hands. Inch by inch, she worked her way down his neck, onto his shoulders. There was a pause while her hands briefly left him. When they returned, her fingers slicked more freely on his skin. The massage oil felt like heaven. He heard himself groan.

"How do you feel about your punishment now?" she asked quietly.

"Punish me, Doc."

She worked slowly down his back with strong strokes. His eyes were closed, and as he drifted, relaxing images flickered through his mind. He thought of sunshine, and saw the slope of a snow-covered mountain where it met the blue sky. His old life was always there, waiting behind his eyelids to remind him of all he'd lost. He sighed and tried to think of nothing at all but the pressure of Callie's touch.

Inevitably, she approached his waistline with her hands. As she got nearer to the awkward place where normal sensation altered, changing abruptly to something foreign and uncomfortable, he tensed.

She paused, leaving her hands in place, pushing firmly against his skin. "Is this too far down?" she asked.

He cleared his throat. "You're okay right there," he said. "But no farther."

"Gotcha. Turn left at the dragon's tail," she said, referring to his tattoo. "Don't tense up, okay?"

He melted back onto the table, and she worked her hands higher up. When she was safely out of the way of his transition band, she changed her touch to a lighter one. She feathered her fingertips down his sides. It felt damn good. In fact, he felt his nipples began to tingle in a sensual way.

Hank lay very still. Was that intentional? Even as he wondered, her hands went back to a more traditional stroke, fingers working the muscles beneath his skin. He let out a shaky breath. How long had it been since anyone had touched him in a loving way? Eleven months, give or take. Making out with Callie had been the only time anyone's hands had been on his body without adjusting his posture or listening to his heart with a chilly stethoscope.

Jesus. He was fucking starved for it.

Happily, those tricky fingers of hers came back. Again she caressed his sides with a sweet sweep of her hands. He was in serious danger of begging for more. Maybe she knew that, or maybe it was just her idea of relaxing him. Either way, it made him feel like a lightning rod in a thunderstorm.

Again her fingers were light and lovely, grazing the sensitive skin on his sides. Hank kept his breath even and decided that Callie knew exactly what she was doing. She was showing him exactly what he could have had if he hadn't run away. Fine. *I get it, lady.* He almost said it out loud, but when she made another sweep down the edges of his pecs, he decided to just go with it. She was free to make her point, and he was free to enjoy it.

Callie's fingers strayed down his torso again, still feathery and light. He was enjoying himself too much to panic as she worked her way down toward his transition area. But as those fingertips went lower, he wondered if he would have to remind her. All at once, she swept her thumbs through the very top edge of that unruly band of skin, and the sensation caused him to stop breathing. Because instead of discomfort, he felt a tingle so deep and so fine that he had never experienced anything like it.

What the...?

Before he could process his reaction, Callie's fingers retreated to safer territory up his spine. She pressed gently on either side of it, her thumbs trailing along behind. This was the oddest massage he had ever received, and he didn't know what Callie was playing at. But it kicked the snot out of another sweaty session on the parallel bars with Tiny.

Hank took a steadying breath and relaxed into her touch. But, holy hell. She was back, teasing his lower waistline, sweeping her fingers through the top of his sensitive area. And the effect was just the same, if not more intense. This time her touch rounded his sides, too, ending near his belly. And he felt such intense pleasure that he was reminded of the first time a girl ever slid her fingers past the elastic of his underwear and slowly onto the skin of his groin. The single sweep of Callie's fingers had the same effect—the shock and awe of an intimate touch. Unbidden, the image of sixteen-year-old Hannah

Smith's face flashed in his mind, and he bit his lip to keep from laughing. "*Shit…*" he mumbled.

Callie's hands froze on his back. "Do you want me to stop?" she whispered. "Am I making you uncomfortable?"

"Don't you *dare* stop." The words came out more harshly than he'd intended. But…*damn.* He hadn't felt like this in so long. Pleasure for pleasure's sake. It was intoxicating.

Callie's warm fingers worked their way back up to his neck. Then his tricky masseuse leaned over his back until some of her hair grazed his shoulder. She put her lips on the nape of his neck. Her kiss was slow, her tongue tasting him. While he held his breath, she dropped her lips near his ear. "I won't do that again. But I just need you to know that I care about you. And there's no hard feelings."

Hank screwed his eyes shut against a flood of emotion. He loved Callie's sensual touch, and he was sorry he'd hurt her. And he wished things were different. There was only one way he could think of to tell her. Lifting one arm off the table, he caught her by the back of her neck, bringing her mouth down to his own. He made the kiss wet and aggressive, sliding his tongue into her mouth, leaving no room for misunderstanding.

Callie made a sexy little noise of surprise. For a moment, she kissed him back. But then she gently extracted herself, going back to work on his spine. Hank took another steadying breath. Whether she knew it or not, Callie was taking him apart. He was miserable about his life, and the fact that he couldn't have her. He had a grim view of his future. But at that very moment, it all mattered a little less. Right now, in this room, under the friction of her hands, all was well. Her generous touch was enough.

He sank into the darkness of his eyelids again. The only

sound was the thud of his own blood in his ears, and the sweet sound of Callie's breathing as she worked. The apple scent of her shampoo enveloped him as she leaned down again, putting her lips on his neck for a second time. Softly, she kissed down his back, her hands sweeping luxurious circles in her wake. When she reached the crazy, lusty erogenous zone formerly known as his waist, she used her fingernails to scratch lightly. And the feel of it almost shot him through the ceiling.

Then, she lowered her mouth to the same area, and began to drop soft, open-mouthed kisses there. And Hank let out a sound that could only be interpreted as an erotic moan.

She picked up her pace a bit, kissing a hot line up his back. When she got nearer to his face, she took his earlobe into her mouth and sucked.

"*Fuck...*" he bit out as she went back to her teasing of his waist. His breathing became shallow and erratic. He found himself rolling his hips from side to side, and realized the urge to do that came from pressure in his groin. The good kind of pressure.

Callie had given him—of all people—a giant woody, and she'd done it by touching his back. It was so trippy. Her fingers were now farther down his waist than he would have thought possible. Whenever a doctor or a rehab nurse had touched him there, it had been monstrously uncomfortable. But Callie's sneak attack had brought on only intense, uncontrolled arousal —the kind he'd felt when he was a teenager looking at *Playboy*.

Unbelievable.

And then she did it *again*, her fingernails dancing across his midsection, stoking the fire. And the sound he made could have been part of the soundtrack for a porn flick.

She bent near his ear again, and he received another slow kiss. Then she said, "You can touch yourself, if you want."

He hesitated only long enough to convince himself that he'd heard her correctly. Then, rolling slightly to the side, he plunged his hand down into his shorts, wrapping his fingers around the impressive erection he found there. While Callie worked her fingernails down his sides, he stroked himself. His fingers trembling, he reached lower, giving his balls a gentle squeeze. Then Callie nibbled his waist, and he couldn't stand it anymore. Pressing his shoulders off the table, he dropped his head forward with a shuddering groan. It seemed to happen in slow motion. His hips shook with pleasure, and hot semen began to spill into his hand. For the first time in almost a year.

Callie's hands stilled.

After two beats of his pulse, he collapsed back onto the table, his exhale a gust into the crook of his arm. There was absolute silence for a moment, and he could hear only his own breathing, and the pounding of his heart. "What the hell just happened here?" he gasped, the words muffled.

She cleared her throat. "If you don't know, then I feel sorry for all your old girlfriends."

He let out a half of a barked laugh, but left his face hidden safely in his elbow. He couldn't show his face, or any of the emotions that were probably written on it—shock, pleasure, relief. And a heavy helping of embarrassment.

He heard the sound of paper towel tearing, and the sink running. Callie placed a damp towel on the corner of the table near his hand. Then she brushed a hand lightly across his head in a gesture of warmth. After that, he heard her footsteps retreating as she left the therapy room.

The door clicked closed, and she did not return.

CHAPTER
ELEVEN

THE HIGH THAT Callie got from making Hank... er... *happy* dissipated surprisingly quickly. Her condo was just as silent and lonely as it usually was when she arrived home.

Furthermore, her old friend mortification crept in under the door.

What on *earth* had she been thinking?

She'd walked into the therapy room with the intention of making Hank feel relaxed and appreciated. When Tiny had massaged her shoulders so beautifully the day before, it had made Callie realize how infrequently she was touched with loving hands. It was a logical leap to assume that Hank was in the same lonely boat.

But then, as she'd touched him, he'd begun to stretch and react under her fingers. That's when she'd let things get out of control. Watching him respond in such a sensual way, she'd gotten drunk on her own power. The moment she'd kissed his neck, a line had been crossed. She hadn't planned to do that. But it had been so gratifying to make the man who'd disappointed her respond.

So much for selflessness.

She'd taken things from sweet to sexy inside of ten minutes flat. Hell, there were probably porn movies that started the way that encounter had. The unsuspecting man lays down on the massage table, and then…

Ugh.

Again she'd strayed way too far outside her comfort zone, and would now have to bear the uncomfortable consequences. Callie had always thought of herself as an intelligent person. But lately there was a startling amount of evidence to the contrary. Hank made her into a bumbling fool. That had been true since the very first time she'd been introduced to him.

As her brain circled endlessly around this spectacular lapse in judgment, she began to worry about the fallout. Hank wasn't going to tell on her. He just wasn't that kind of guy. But what if someone saw her kissing a patient? Not *her* patient, of course. But that wasn't the kind of detail that would shine through if the story ever made the front page of the local newspaper, would it? *Local Doctor Molests Patient. Film at eleven.*

Film. Did the hospital have security cameras in the therapy room? The very idea made Callie spring up off her sofa and head to the kitchen for a glass of wine. "I am the world's biggest idiot." Callie spoke this sentence aloud, and her condo was so still that the words practically echoed right back to her.

Counting up every move Hank had made didn't reassure her. Because *she* was the doctor. She had a duty to him and not the other way around.

Callie fell into a distracted funk, and didn't sleep well for the next several nights. Her conscience shamed her late into the night. And it didn't matter that there was a contradicting voice, a tiny one, which pointed out that she'd made Hank feel good, and that he'd needed that.

What she did was still not okay. And she heard it like a drum beat in her head. *Not okay. Not okay.*

Meanwhile, her work schedule was grueling. After spending yet another busy day at the hospital, she came home to her condo one night to find Hank sitting on the bench outside.

She tried to keep her face from falling, but she was too spent for polite conversation.

"Hi," he said quickly. "Got a minute?"

Not really. Callie hoped he hadn't been waiting long, because she really needed to do a face-plant on her sofa right now. "What's up?" she said, sitting down beside him.

"Well," his voice was low. "Last time I came to apologize to you, it didn't go so well. So I just wanted to tell you again how sorry I am that I embarrassed you before. You have no idea how highly I think of you." He chuckled nervously. "Well, after last Friday, maybe you do."

Callie withheld a sigh. "We don't have to talk about it anymore. I told you—no hard feelings."

He reached over to her hand where it lay on the bench, massaging it briefly with his warm palm. "I know you did. But I still want you to understand. The reaction I had the other day… Things don't usually work that well for me. I was awake half the night trying to convince myself that it actually happened."

Callie needed to extract herself from this conversation and go inside. "You know, there are specialists who deal with this all the time. I'll bet most of the guys in the therapy program see a urologist."

"I know. I already made the appointment." A silence settled over them, but it was not unpleasant. After a few moments he spoke again. "Right after my injury, my girlfriend dumped me. I went from being a…" He paused.

"Man whore?" she supplied.

He rolled his eyes. "I prefer 'player.' Anyway, I went from the guy girls threw their panties at, to the guy who couldn't keep it up. My girlfriend dumped me when I still had a catheter up my…" He glanced up at her. "She said, 'I'm an athlete, and I need a real man,' and she took off."

"How old was she?"

"Twenty-four."

"And were you a paragon of wisdom at twenty-four?"

"Only when I was stoned."

Callie sighed. "So you let a twenty-four-year-old witch convince you that you're no longer a sexual being?"

"Well, when you put it *that* way…" He sighed, too. "Look, I just wanted to tell you again that I'm sorry things went so wrong between us. I don't have a high tolerance for humiliation."

Callie felt the sting of inconvenient tears threaten at the back of her throat. "*Funny,* but neither do I."

He cleared his throat. "I know. I'm sorry I ever caused you any."

"I know you are. But you're not the only one sitting here who was recently dumped, and told they weren't sexy enough anymore."

His eyes got wide. "Who would say that to you?"

"My live-in boyfriend was a doctor at the hospital." She looked away. "I caught him cheating on me with a nursing student."

"Wait…that skinny dude with the glasses? The one who asked you to cover his shift?"

She shrugged.

"Hang on, girl. So this little shit got caught in the act. If he said you weren't all that, he only did it to try to share the blame. He's a coward, Callie. I hope you told him so."

"Not really. Instead, I just carried around the echo of his words in my head. But I still..." She swallowed. "I was still willing to go there with you. And look how that turned out."

"I did not *reject* you, Callie."

"I know you believe that. But if you could try to put yourself in someone else's shoes, you'd see how it looked to me."

"Shit. I'm sorry, okay? I was afraid."

"I know you were. And now so am I. So, thanks for that." Her voice quavered as she said it, and his face fell. "I've been at work for twelve hours, Hank. I'm too tired to have this conversation in a way that doesn't end in..." She almost said *tears.* "...Me being crabby," she said instead.

Hank grabbed her hand and raised it to his lips. He kissed her palm gently. "Do you have any days this week when you aren't working twelve hours? Because I'd really like to take you out to dinner."

Callie's insides swooped and then dove. "I can't say *yes,*" she said in a small voice. "It wouldn't be ethical for me to date a patient in the therapy program. I shouldn't have ever..." She cleared her throat. "What I did the other day... That was wrong."

His face fell. "That can't be true. Because what you did the other day gave me something I haven't felt in a long time. You took me out of my head and shook me up. And it really sucks to hear that you feel bad about it now."

Callie felt a lump in her throat the size of New England. Because it occurred to her that there was something else at work here. Maybe Hank was attracted to her only *because* she was a doctor. Who would a paralyzed man turn to if he needed help understanding how his post-crash body worked? A doctor. And preferably one who had just read everything on the planet about paralysis.

"I should go," Callie whispered. "I'll see you at the hospital."

She chanced a look at his face, and then immediately wished that she hadn't. Because the regret in those deep brown eyes was soul-deep. "Take care of yourself, Callie girl."

"You, too," she said with a hard swallow. Then she walked away.

CHAPTER
TWELVE

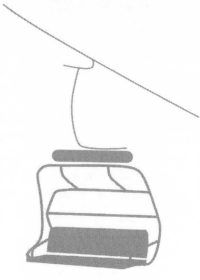

IN HANK'S DREAMS, there was never a need for a wheelchair. When his eyes were shut, moving under his own power was easy again. Now, Hank dreamed of walking the hospital corridors, which didn't make any sense, because he'd never been there until he could no longer walk.

But that was the way of dreams.

He passed through to the men's locker room, and then beyond, to the pool-deck door. He stepped into the steamy, chlorinated room. The place was largely deserted, the water in the therapy pool glassy. But a single figure sat alone in the hot tub. A certain doctor relaxed there, her head tipped back, eyes closed.

The only sound was the burble of water as Hank walked to the edge of the tub. When he put a hand on the side to climb in, she opened her eyes.

Wordlessly, Hank slipped into the water. And just as easily, he drew Callie against his body and began to kiss her. This being a dream, no discussion was really necessary. And when she climbed onto his body, straddling him, he realized that neither of them was wearing any clothes. There was only heated, slippery skin against aroused skin. With a groan, Hank leaned into the curves of her body. Reaching for her, trying to get more of her into his arms, Hank…

Woke up.

Blinking in his sunlit bedroom, he took stock of the situation. Callie was nowhere to be found. A week had passed since their depressing conversation, and his dreams were the only place he'd seen her lately. He had to hand it to his subconscious, though. The hot tub was a nice touch. Too bad the only accurate detail from the whole dream was his lack of clothing. Hank had always enjoyed sleeping in the nude, and breaking his back had not changed that habit.

Hank lifted the covers and cast an eye down his body. His penis looked up at him, mostly erect and jutting over his belly. Dropping the sheets back into place, Hank lay still for a moment. There was no place he had to be today. It would be easy to just close his eyes and drowse for a while longer.

Instead, he slid one tentative hand down his body and stroked himself. Immediately the doubts began to kick in. This probably wouldn't work. And when he went soft in a few minutes, it was going to depress the hell out of him. Again.

Heaving a sigh, he withdrew his hand.

There was an irony at work here. Before his accident, teaching his body new tricks had been practically all that Hank did all day. To be a freestyle snowboarder was to constantly hurl yourself into the air, scrambling to achieve that extra half rotation into the trick before gravity won. When Hank had been working on a new trick, he always crashed dozens of times before he made it work. And then as soon as the trick became part of his repertoire, he'd choose some new punishing feat and get to work on it.

Crash. Get up. Crash. Try again. He'd been doing that since he got his first snowboard at age seven. Even during those rare times when he was visited by doubts, he didn't quit. Because noodling with his snowboard was what he did. Stopping would not even have been possible.

For the first time in his life, a physical challenge had him tied in knots.

Hank sat up in bed. Tapping the phone dock beside his bed, he started a Pearl Jam playlist. Now there was a mood lifter. Transferring to his chair, he wheeled into the bathroom. But instead of starting the shower, Hank opened a drawer in the vanity and removed a blister pack with colorful tablets in it. The urologist had given it to him two days ago. Extracting one from the package, he studied the pill. The idea that anything so small could solve his problem was pretty ridiculous. But the doctor had been very encouraging. "It's like gas on the accelerator," he'd said. "I'll be stunned if these don't help you."

Hank tossed the pill in his mouth and then drank a glass of water.

But now what? The pill needed half an hour to take effect. He rolled back into the bedroom, where Eddie Vedder was singing "Black" from the excellent stereo speakers he'd added during the renovation. Tossing himself onto the bed, Hank stretched out. He dropped his hand between his legs and cupped his sack. Closing his eyes, he called up the dream he'd been having. The warm water. Callie's naked body.

Just relax, he ordered himself. The doctor had also said not to worry if he didn't get the reaction he wanted on the first try.

Hank took a deep breath and sank back onto the bed. Getting comfortable, he exhaled, quieting his mind.

"Hazardous, are you back here?"

Even as his brain registered his sister's voice, a knock came on the bedroom door.

Hank yanked up the covers. "Stella? I'm getting dressed."

Her voice was muffled by the door. "I came to take you to brunch with Mom. Please, will you come with us?"

"Mom is here?" Hank turned off the music. Then he transferred to his chair and began to get dressed.

"No, she's meeting me at the Maplewood Inn, and I was hoping you'd come with us. I should have called, I know."

Hank zipped up his jeans very carefully. Though his sister's timing was awful, he couldn't deny that he was happy to hear from her. His little sister hadn't stopped by in ages. And if she wanted to drag him to brunch, then he was game.

He rolled over to his closet and opened the door. "Hey, Stella? Can you come in here a second and find me a shirt that says 'brunch with Mom.'"

She opened the door and gave him a once over. "Jeans?"

He shrugged. "I'm going along to absorb some of Mom's disapproval, Stell. What do you care what I'm wearing? Besides, this is Vermont. There's no dress code. Even at the Maplewood."

"Don't get your panties in a bunch." Stella stepped around his chair and picked through the shirts. "I just need to know so I can choose the right thing. I've always liked this." She held out a black shirt cut from some kind of sueded moleskin cloth for his approval.

He beckoned with two fingers, and she unbuttoned it from the hanger, tossing it to him when she was done.

"Socks?" she asked, walking toward his dresser and opening the bottom drawer.

"I'll get 'em. You don't have to baby me." Although it hadn't been long ago when Hank had been so laid up that people were actually dressing him. Not a fun memory. He buttoned the shirt, taking care to leave it untucked and hanging down over his crotch, just in case the pill he'd taken was more effective than he bargained for.

"I'm not babying you. I'm *rushing* you. That's different."

"Good to know."

"Hank?" She paused with her hand on his bedroom door. "Thanks for coming with me on, like, zero notice. I know you're not just sitting around, eating bonbons."

Ah, but it was nearly true these days. He was either at the hospital or here. But didn't that sound pathetic? "Lucky for you, I'm free," he said. "And starved." But that wasn't really the reason he'd hopped to when Stella came through the door. It had been a long time since his little sister sought out his company.

Right after the accident, Stella had been great. And when she'd eventually stopped coming around, Hank had assumed she had her own life to lead, and needed to get on with it. So he hadn't thrown any guilt her way, or made a big deal about it. But after their little chat at Rupert's, he should have realized that she was hurting, too.

"Should I start the car?" she asked. "Mom is such a freak about being prompt."

"I'm doing my best here, babe." He propped up his leg on the bed and put his sock on. "Hey—is there any background dirt that you want me to have before we get there? Are you still lobbying Mom about your trip to Valdez?"

She gave her head a sad little shake. "I've given up, honestly. She wants me to sit out a year. But that's just code for hoping I find something more worthy to do with my time."

It sucked that his sister's life was in as much flux as his

own. What a shitty year they'd had. "Have you talked to Bear, by any chance?"

His sister's face did something weird then. A peculiar flash of dismay crossed her features, before she chased it away again. Stella cleared her throat. "Bear? Why?"

"He wants to make a film. He was trying to get me to narrate it, but I turned him down. Anyway, he mentioned heli-skiing, so I know he was thinking about big mountain shots. Maybe he's going somewhere you haven't been yet."

A moment went by before she answered. "Wow. Okay."

"Actually, I'm supposed to see him next weekend. He was going to pass me some of the details. I'll ask then."

"Thanks," she whispered.

"You're welcome, sweetie. I know Mom is cramping your style, and it's all because of me."

"That's not your fault, though," she said, her voice low. "Hank, I'm sorry I haven't been around."

Aw. He hadn't meant to give her a guilt trip. "Come here." Stella walked close to him, and Hank pulled her down for a hug. "We're still on the same team, right?"

"Always," she whispered, wrapping her arms around his shoulders.

Hank gave her a squeeze. He'd been so distracted by his own misery lately that there hadn't been any room for Stella's troubles. But it had been juvenile of him not to see that his injury had hurt everyone at the same time.

"Glad to have you back," he said, his voice gruff. "Now, let's get Mom to buy us an overpriced breakfast. Can you grab my keys off the hook?"

"Can I drive your Porsche?"

"Never," came Hank's quick reply.

"Damn it."

CHAPTER
THIRTEEN

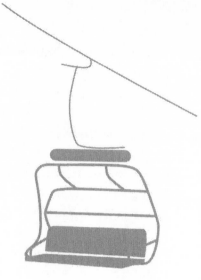

THE FOLLOWING SUNDAY, Callie drove toward the hospital, past the scarecrows and the pumpkin patches. It was a perfect sunny Vermont day, and almost sixty degrees outside. But the gorgeous weather made her feel grim. She was on her way to work yet again, subbing a half shift for none other than Nathan. She should have turned him down on principle, but she had nothing better to do. And there was always the over-time pay to cheer her. Callie's student-loan account flourished even while her social life was as dry as the Indian corn decorating doors all over Vermont.

Traffic slowed on the approach into town, and Callie realized why when she saw tents set up on the town green. Today was the annual harvest festival. Braking to a stop to allow a departing car to slide into traffic in front of her, Callie realized that a piece of homemade pie might cheer her up. She had twenty minutes to spare before her shift, so she nabbed the newly vacant parking spot and killed the engine. If the line wasn't too long, she could even listen to the band for a few minutes, or check out the used-book sale.

The festival was a big deal in tiny Hamilton, and so the food tent was packed. Callie paid for a piece of apple pie with crumb topping, then tried to thread her way toward the outdoors. Her progress was halted by a tall man who had managed to trip on something. For a moment, Callie thought he was going to end up face-first on the grass. But he recovered, muttered a hasty apology to someone in the crowd and scurried off.

When he moved away, Callie realized that the thing he'd tripped on was a wheelchair. And its occupant, complete with hot, mirrored shades on his face, sexy stubble on his jaw and familiar tattoos on his arms, was looking right at her.

Crap. Too late for evasive maneuvers.

She forced a smile on her face. "Hi there."

"Hi yourself." Hank tossed an empty plate into a garbage bin and wheeled to face her. "Come here often?"

Callie couldn't help but grin at his ironic use of a cheesy pickup line. "Sure. You?"

Hank lifted his chin toward the other side of the green. "My friend Bear is here somewhere—I told him I'd come and find him. Want to walk with me?"

"For a few minutes," Callie said, happy to have an excuse to step away soon, even if it was a lame one. "I'm working a four-hour stint as a favor to someone. But I couldn't drive by apple pie on the way to the hospital."

"All right. Eat your pie, and then I'll introduce you to Bear."

Together, they paused on the edge of the crowd in front of the band shell, where a vocalist was delivering an earnest version of a Dave Matthews hit. Callie polished off her slice and enjoyed the feeling of the sun on her face. She had the hottest man in Vermont at her side. Even if there was a strain between them, life could always be worse. When the song ended, she pitched her empty plate into a garbage receptacle. "I should probably get to work soon, with the other losers."

"Come and meet my friend first, before you slap that *L* onto your forehead." Hank winked. He wheeled away, toward the quieter side of the festivities, and Callie trotted along beside him. "Bear was on the competition circuit with me," Hank said. "Now he wants to be a filmmaker. The State of Vermont hired him to shoot an ad for next year's foliage season."

"Well, that's pretty cool," Callie said.

"He thinks so. That will be him, behind that cart full of pumpkins," Hank said.

When they rounded a picturesque wooden wagon and a horse, Callie spied a beautiful young woman, a blonde, sitting on a hay bale while another woman bent over her with a powder puff. At the sight of them, Hank's face closed up tight. When the pretty girl turned her chin a few degrees, Callie recognized her. She was the girlfriend who had cried her eyes out in the hospital corridor all those months ago.

She was the one who dumped Hank after the accident.

Hank let go of his wheels, coming to a quick stop.

Then, a brawny, bearded guy came trotting toward them. "Big man! I'm happy to see you." He stopped in front of them, a smile on his face and a question in his eyes when he looked at Callie.

"Hi," she volunteered. "I'm Callie."

"Sorry," Hank said, snapping out of his stupor. "Callie, this is my friend Bear. Bear, Callie is a friend from the hospital."

Callie and Bear shook hands, but Hank's face was still stonelike. "So what's with...?" He cocked a head toward the blonde.

Bear looked guilty. "I guess I forgot to mention she would be in town."

"Funny," Hank muttered. "I didn't feel a disturbance in the force."

There was a silence, over which they could all hear the grating pitch of the girl's voice. "Watch it with the blue eye shadow," she snipped at the makeup lady. "This isn't 1975."

But Callie could see that even the worst makeup job would still leave the irritable girl looking ravishing. How was it even fair that a top female athlete could also have the sexy pout of a model?

In comparison, Callie was downright dowdy. And the realization was bracing to her. The blonde was the sort of girl that Hank was used to dating. Only last month he had said that he was sick of adjusting his expectations, to accepting that everything in his life from now on would be second rate.

If Callie had needed a way to stop yearning for him, this was it. She never wanted to become anyone's adjust-your-expectations girlfriend. She didn't need to be Hank's distant second.

The girl stood up, turning to face them. When she caught sight of Hank, a smile lit her face. Before Callie could make her excuses and run, the girl was already bounding toward them.

"Hank!" she cried, running up to kiss him on the cheek. "You look good. How *are* you?" Straightening up, she stood right smack in front of his chair. That required Hank to crane his neck to look up at her.

"Thanks, Alexis. I'm doing all right," he muttered. Callie could see him fighting the urge to wheel backward a few feet, leveling his chin and therefore the playing field.

A tense silence settled between them, and Callie wished she'd already made her exit. Poor Hank was having his own double-awkward moment. And was that rock on the girl's finger her engagement ring?

"Callie has to take off," Hank said. "So we'll just..." He nodded toward the parking lot.

"But you just got here," Alexis insisted. "Tell me everything, Hank. Are you coming out West when Bear shoots his film?"

"Um, not sure about that." Meeting Callie's eyes, he tried for a smile but it didn't quite work.

Alexis tossed her hair. "Park City has been a little quiet this year. Everybody is pulling back a bit after last year's schedule. Olympic season is always *so* exhausting." Her smile was wide, but Callie had to wonder if she'd brought up the Olympics to purposely wound Hank, or if she was just that insensitive. To make matters worse, the tension in the air was ratcheted up by a sudden torrent of crying from a toddler somewhere just behind Callie. Alexis licked her lips with what looked like nerves, and so Callie decided to give her the benefit of the doubt. But then she said something that was less than endearing. "Why is that kid screaming? God. Someone shut her up."

Callie turned her head to find the source of the trouble. A young family was standing just fifteen feet away. The mother held the screaming toddler in her arms. The little girl, maybe two years old, held on to her left wrist with her chubby right hand. Her shrieks were high-pitched in a way that suggested pain.

"I was just swinging her around," the dad said, his face reddening. "You know, in a circle. And she started hollering like that." He reached over and took the little girl from his wife, bouncing her on his hip in a soothing way. But the little girl only cried harder, still clenching that wrist.

Even as her ears began to hurt, Callie realized that while

some problems in the world were difficult to fix, that family's problem was not among them.

Callie left Hank and his friends to cross the lawn toward the wailing toddler. "Excuse me." She smiled as warmly as she could at the strained parents. "Has your daughter ever dislocated her elbow before?"

The father winced as the little girl screamed too near his ear. He shook his head.

Callie pointed at the little girl's arms. "A dislocated elbow hurts at the wrist, and children will often hold it like that. I'm a doctor, and I've seen this in the E.R. before. May I touch her?"

Both parents nodded vigorously, as their daughter continued to show off her great pair of lungs.

Gently, Callie took the little girl's hurt arm in her own hand. There were tears streaming down her little face. Still crying, she watched Callie but did not seem to mind the intervention. In one fluid motion, Callie rolled the chubby wrist over so that her hand was palm up. Then she gently bent the little arm at the elbow, bringing her palm up near her shoulder. Then Callie repeated this action—rolling the hand and bending the arm.

The little girl went suddenly silent, cutting off her shrieking right in the middle of a scream. Half a beat later, both parents' shoulders relaxed.

"Squeeze my hand," Callie said to the little girl. The child reached out. "No...silly! With this other one." She pointed to the formerly dislocated arm.

The little girl reached for Callie and squeezed.

"Oh, my God, thank you!" the mother gushed. The father just stared, his jaw dropped in surprise.

"It's called nursemaid's elbow. It happens all the time," Callie said quickly. "Some kids are more prone to it than others, though. Take care not to tug on her arm at all for a while—maybe two weeks. It will be vulnerable for a repeat incident."

The dad just shook his head. "I'll never twirl her in the air again."

The poor guy's guilt was palpable. "I know, right?" Callie winked at him. "No good deed goes unpunished."

The little family made more noises of gratitude, but if Callie didn't get to work right now, she'd be late. "My pleasure," she said.

When she turned around again, the first thing she saw was Hank, who was watching her. He winked.

Callie should have run over to say goodbye to him. But it would probably only be awkward. Instead, she pointed at her watch, and then toward the parking lot. Then she made the sign of an L with her fingers and held it up to her forehead.

He nodded, his smile warm. She gave him a little wave then walked away. As she strode for her car, Callie saw the young family she'd helped get in line for a maple creemee soft serve.

Well at least I'm good for something, Callie thought as she dug her keys from her pocket.

At the hospital, Callie found Nathan in the break room, bent over a copy of the Sunday crossword puzzle. "Hey!" he said, smiling up at her. "The fabric's edge. Seven letters."

"Selvage," Callie said immediately. Without thinking, she pulled out the other chair and sat down opposite him. They'd always done the crossword together. God, she really missed having someone else in her life. The little rituals of coupledom had soothed her, and made her feel useful.

"I was never coming up with that on my own," Nathan admitted, inking it in. "How about Pavarotti's birthplace? I tried Verona, but the V can't be right."

Callie closed her eyes. "Modena?"

"Ah!" he scribbled. "You are a total babe."

For a half second, this crumb of a compliment lit her up. But then Nathan pushed his chair back and stood up. "I have to go. Thanks for coming in. It's been quiet so far."

"Don't you dare jinx me by using the Q word," Callie warned.

Nathan gave her a sad smile. "Sorry."

Callie shook off her disappointment and pulled on a lab coat. "If you don't have any charts to show me, you can take off. More wedding plans?"

His smile fell away. "Nope. I'm taking my mother out for a late lunch to tell her that the wedding is off."

"What?" Callie couldn't even hide her surprise.

He shook his head, his eyes on the floor. "Shelli dumped me for a younger doctor up at Hitchcock. Hit me with all the 'I told you so's' that you want."

No shit? Nathan's admission was startling. It took super-human strength, but Callie bit back all the obvious comments. "I'm sorry for your troubles, Nathan."

"Yeah, well. I brought them on myself."

Callie found that she suddenly didn't have anything to do with her eyes. Her phone had buzzed from inside her bag several times in the past half hour, so Callie chose that moment to peer at it.

She had a voice mail and two texts, all of them from

Willow. *Call me,* read the first text. And *I have a SURPRISE!* read the second one. Hmm…a surprise?

"Callie?"

She looked up to see Nathan standing right in front of her. Before she could even process his movements, he stepped right into her personal space and kissed her gently on the lips. "I'm sorry I was an ass." Too startled to speak, Callie just stood there, staring at him.

Nathan put his hands on her shoulders and gave them a squeeze. "I'm sorry," he said again. "I threw away what we had for…a diversion. It was the stupidest thing I've ever done."

"What are you saying?" Callie asked, her voice roughened by surprise.

"I should have known that Shelli and I wouldn't be together for the long haul." His chuckle sounded nervous. "You know—turning thirty, thinking nothing exciting would ever happen to me again. I felt like I'd spent my life in a lab coat."

Callie gave her head a little toss, trying to shake off her stupor. "We're having the same midlife crisis," she admitted at a whisper.

Nathan smiled then, and his face was more vulnerable and open at that moment than she'd ever seen it. "Want to have it together?" he asked.

Without waiting for an answer, Nathan put his hand beneath Callie's chin. He tipped her face up to meet his, and the kiss she received was warm and slow. Callie felt herself go absolutely still, taking in the moment with every cell of her being. She'd waited a long time for this—for Nathan to reverse the nightmare of his sudden rejection. It had taken so long that Callie had truly stopped expecting it to happen. What she felt right now was more surprise than glee.

Instead of losing herself in the kiss, she got sidetracked by the realization that vindication was not as sexy as it ought to be. Worse, a certain set of coal-dark eyes and sculpted shoulder muscles rose up from somewhere deep in her subconscious. And with it came the very ache of disappointment that Nathan had once inspired.

Callie stepped back, breaking the kiss. "No," she gasped. "Nathan, I can't do this."

"Why?"

She didn't even know what to say. "I'm hung up on someone else. So this wouldn't be fair to you or me." That was the truth, even if she and Hank had no future together. To be with Nathan right now would be settling for something lesser.

His eyes went wide. "Callie, we were good together. You said so yourself."

"You ended it," she whispered, "almost two years ago now. I've moved on." *I tried to, anyway.*

Silent, Nathan stood twisting his watch on his wrist for a moment. And then all at once he grabbed his jacket off the chair and left the room.

Callie sagged into a chair, trying to figure out what had just happened. *We were good together.* At the time she'd said it all those months ago, she'd believed it. Maybe it was even true. It's just that "good" wasn't as compelling as it used to be. And that little germ of an idea—a tiny cell—dug its way into her consciousness. The whole encounter with Nathan certainly invited reflection. But she would have to do that later. Because there were rounds to make, and medications to review.

With a flustered shake of her head, Callie donned her lab coat and got to work.

At the end of her shift, Callie took a moment to herself on a hospital computer. She logged in to her personal email for the first time all day. And when she saw Marin Hospital in the subject line of a new message, her stomach gave a nervous little kick. "Dear Dr. Anders, It was with great interest that we read your cover letter. Unfortunately…" Callie's stomach took a dive when she read that word. Why did every exciting thing in her life always come around to the word *unfortunately*? But as she read on, she saw that it wasn't so bad.

Unfortunately, we have a hiring freeze through the end of the calendar year. We expect the restriction to end on January 1, however. If in the meantime you could forward your transcripts to Dr. Johnston, we will put you at the top of our interview list come January.

Well. That was progress. Callie logged off the computer, mindful that she didn't want anyone from her current employer to know that she was considering a job change.

But that would be a problem, wouldn't it? If she were forwarding her transcripts to a hospital in California, they were going to notice. And she couldn't wait too long to get the process started, because getting a license to practice in California took weeks. Maybe months.

People changed jobs all the time, of course. It's just that her FES study had ten months left to go. However she made her departure, it would have to be done in such a way that the baton passed smoothly. And since Hank had made her participation one of his stipulations, Callie would have to let him know her decision, and ask him to be gracious about the switch. After everything that had happened between them, she was confident he wouldn't make too much of a fuss. He was too good a guy.

Damn. She had to stop thinking warm cuddly thoughts about him.

The thing to do would be to let Hank know first. It wouldn't be easy, but once she'd ripped off that proverbial bandage, she'd feel freer to plan the next chapter of her life.

At the end of her shift, Callie retrieved her jacket from her locker. Walking toward the exit doors, she passed Dr. Fennigan walking in. "Callie!" the older woman called. "How has your weekend been?" She winked in acknowledgment of the fact that both of them were standing here on hospital property, instead of somewhere more relaxing.

"Um, well! It's going well." She felt jittery, as if Dr. Fennigan would be able to read off her face that she was planning to defect to the West Coast.

"Glad to hear it. I ran into Hank Lazarus at the harvest festival earlier."

"Oh?" A guilty blush broke over her skin. Callie's sins with Hank were far worse than plotting to jump ship. If Dr. Fennigan knew what had transpired between them, she might even encourage her to interview elsewhere.

"He said you fixed some poor child's wrist on the green today."

"It was only…"

"…Nursemaid's elbow," Dr. Fennigan finished. "I figured as much. But Mr. Lazarus thinks you performed a miracle. He gets a certain look on his face when he talks about you, honestly." The older woman was smiling now, and Callie felt herself break into a sweat. "Good thing you two don't have a doctor-patient relationship."

What?

Face aflame, Callie forced herself to meet Dr. Fennigan's eyes. That little statement piqued her interest like nothing else the doctor had ever said to her. But something wouldn't let her ask for clarification. After the mess she'd made for herself already, it was just too risky.

The director winked. "I'd better get going. Apparently, there are two or three fires that need putting out even before the week begins." Laying a hand on Callie's arm, she bid her good-night.

Her mind spinning, Callie walked outside, where it was already dark. The crisp air held the dry scent of decaying leaves. Vermont was a beautiful place, but Callie knew that it was time to let go. She dug her phone and pager out of her bag. Willow's messages were waiting. She ought to reply, but Callie would call her after this difficult discussion was done.

Instead, Callie keyed Hank's number into her phone before she lost her nerve. If he was home, she'd tell him about her career dilemma tonight, before she lost her nerve.

CHAPTER
FOURTEEN

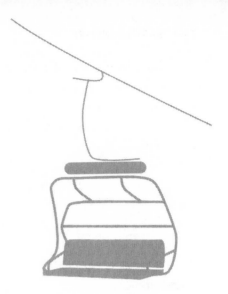

AFTER TAKING Callie's unexpected call, Hank was pretty damned happy that he'd spent the afternoon cleaning up his house. He had no idea what she wanted to talk to him about, but he'd encouraged her to come over, anyway.

Hank adjusted the volume on his living-room stereo, and checked the supply of firewood. Since he was expecting guests later, he'd tried to make the place look cheerier and less lonely than it usually did. There were several kinds of beer in the fridge and a pot of chili simmering on a back burner.

While he'd been spiffing up the place, Hank had also spent the past few hours replaying the scene at the harvest festival in his mind. Damn Alexis. Did a more shallow person exist? It caused him almost physical pain to realize how many months he'd spent brooding over her. What a waste.

When they were dating, the only nice words out of Alexis's mouth were moaned in bed. The rest of the time she'd spent complaining.

Until today, he'd forgotten.

He didn't even need a side-by-side comparison to know

that Callie was twice the woman Alexis was. While Alexis had shot off her mouth about the screaming little kid, Callie had walked over and *fixed* it, like some kind of brainy, busty superhero. It made Hank smile just to remember it. Callie was the whole package, tied up in a bow.

He'd probably blown his chance. Except now she was on her way to his house, with something she wanted to say to him. He had no clue what it was. But he would make her a drink and listen.

And look for an opening.

Whistling to himself, Hank wheeled past the kitchen and into the master suite. As he entered his generously sized handicapped bathroom, his own face greeted him in the mirror. Instead of looking away, as he usually did, Hank gave himself the once-over. And it wasn't entirely bad news. All the extra physical therapy was starting to show in the form of added muscle. And his color was better than it had been since before his accident.

How strange to see the old Hank looking back at him, when he didn't really feel like the same person. But the mirror didn't know that. Apart from the wheelchair, he looked like the guy who was about to throw a snowboard in his old SUV, and jet off to Breckenridge or Tahoe.

Hank opened up his medicine cabinet. Outside, he heard the sound of tires on the gravel drive. The knock on the front door came while he was still rummaging through his medications.

"Come in," he called. "I'll just be a minute." He heard the door open.

"Take your time," a sweet voice called.

Hank found the pill he'd been looking for. He pressed it

out of the bubble pack and dropped it into his palm. It lay there, the brightly colored coating winking up at him.

If at first, you don't succeed...

It was easier to spout clichés than to defeat his fears. But since when was a physical challenge so intimidating? You were supposed to fall on your ass a hundred times before the trick became solid. And as soon as you mastered it, you started in on the next thing. Hank brought the pill up to his mouth and dry swallowed it.

The problem was, when you bombed a snowboarding trick, you could hurt yourself pretty bad. Hank knew that better than anybody. But when you crashed in the bedroom, there were other people who got hurt, too. It was complicated as all hell, and he hated that. But still, it was worth the risk. The good stuff always was.

Callie used her minute alone to take envious glances at his incredible open-plan home. There was a big stone fireplace in the corner, where a log glowed behind the grate. Nearby, a giant L-shaped sofa framed a cocktail table. Its wooden surface was low and quirky, the rough-hewn planks surrounded by a hammered-steel edge. Everywhere she looked there were masculine, industrial details on display. Behind the living area stretched a long bar, fronting a sleek kitchen. Off to the right, floor-to-ceiling windows wrapped around a dining alcove.

Wow.

From somewhere nearby, hidden speakers emitted the low pulse of music. Beside the door sat a shoe rack. Taking the hint, she toed off her leather clogs just as Hank emerged from a doorway, his shoulders looking so broad and strapping that she wondered how he could fit through the door. Above that, he wore a devastatingly handsome smile. "Well, hi there."

"Hi." Callie returned his smile, feeling self-conscious. "Are you... Do you have company?" She smelled food cooking, and hoped she wasn't interrupting something.

He hesitated for a brief pulse before shaking his head. "No. I was just fixing to make myself a cocktail. Will you have one?"

It was Callie's turn to hesitate. She hadn't meant this to be a social visit. But it didn't have to be an antisocial one. And she wasn't ready to just blurt out her request. *Please don't make trouble for the study if I leave for California.* She took a deep breath. "A drink would be lovely, thanks." She would ask this favor as a friend, and there was no reason why friends shouldn't have a cocktail together.

He turned into his kitchen, reaching up to free a couple glasses from their rack, where they hung under a wall cabinet. It was both accessible and macho. It looked like the setup over Rupert's Bar in town. "We can do a gin and tonic, or beer. Or a snakebite?"

"The snakebite," Callie chose. "I love those."

Hank opened a below-counter refrigerator and took out two bottles. He capped them on a bottle opener affixed to the wall, then carefully split the beer and hard cider between their two glasses. "Why don't you grab these and have a seat," he said. "I'll be right there."

Callie took the glasses and carried them over to the sofa. A minute later he swung into view with a cheese board and crackers. He set the board on the coffee table, then quickly bounced himself from the wheelchair to the sofa beside her. He popped a cracker into his mouth and smiled at her.

She handed him a glass. "Cheers."

They touched glasses, and Callie took a sip, holding his

eyes. She had it again—the sensation that she was in over her head. This sexy man, in his bachelor pad, with those penetrating dark eyes made her feel like she was in seventh grade again. She wasn't used to sitting at the cool kids' table.

He eyed her over the rim of his pint glass while he took a deep drink. "What's on your mind, lady?"

She took another swallow, wondering how best to put it. "Well, a few months ago, just before you shook up my hospital job, there was a change I was just about to make."

He put his elbow on the back of the couch, and propped his head against his hand. His brown eyes bored into hers, and she had the sensation that nobody could listen more closely than he did at that moment. Long after she left Vermont, Callie was sure she'd remember the affecting way he looked at her, as if she were the only person alive.

She plunged onward. "I'm a young doctor, and so recommendations matter a lot. I've been wanting to move to California. But I can't get a job there unless my transcripts are squeaky clean." She took another sip of her drink, the cider and beer together creating a lovely tart flavor that she would always associate with Vermont. Hank regarded her silently, which was beginning to feel unnerving. "So, I was hoping you wouldn't make a fuss if the hospital appoints someone else to run the study. Because I need my boss to keep her funding if I disappear."

There. She'd said it.

Hank kept watching her, and she stared back, trying not to fall into the dark pools of his eyes. Finally he spoke. "You came to tell me you want to move to California."

She nodded. "I've been thinking about it for almost a year."

He didn't say another word, not a single one. Instead, he reached for the glass in her hand. Removing it, he set it on the coffee table. Then he hitched himself closer to her and took her face in both hands. The brown eyes got larger as they approached. And then they fell shut as he brushed her lips with his.

Damn. It. All.

Callie's heart began to pound as Hank's thumb brushed lightly across her jaw. She really ought to pull away. She knew she should. But her body went absolutely still, refusing to move.

His next kiss was as slow and gentle as a whisper. Afterward, they regarded each other silently for a beat, before his lips came down again, slanting soft and moist across hers. His tongue brushed her lower lip, and the sweet slick against her mouth caused her to take a sharp breath. When she opened for him, Hank made a little noise of approval in the back of his throat. It was a cross between a groan and a grunt. But whatever it was, the sound rippled through her body. Without meaning to, Callie leaned in, her body ignoring orders to stay put. The slide of his tongue against hers became insistent, and his firm, full lips pressed their case, convincing Callie to let her guard down.

Damn, but this man could kiss.

She gave herself over to it, reaching for him, yielding to him. The next moment she found herself briefly airborne, as powerful arms lifted her by the hips and onto his lap. She was facing him now, almost straddling him. But there was no time to consider the implications, since his tongue kept up its friendly invasion of her mouth (and, truth be told, of her executive function as well). Meanwhile, Hank's hands skimmed down her back, hovering low on her waist.

To steady herself, Callie put her hands on his chest. But the hard muscle under her palms invited exploration, and she skimmed her fingertips over his pecs and down his sides until he groaned. "Callie," he whispered against her mouth.

But she didn't want to hear what he might say next. Perhaps he was about to suggest they knock it off, or maybe the opposite—he might have been ready to ask permission to take things further. Both options were unsettling. So Callie did the only sensible thing. She wrapped her hands behind his muscular neck and kissed him harder.

Hank didn't argue. He only pulled her closer, those steely arms encircling her with a vice grip. Her breasts grazed his chest, and the friction was crazy-making. And how weird to think that Hank was the second man she'd kissed today. That was a lifetime first. There was absolutely no comparison, either. Hank's kisses were magic.

"Callie," he whispered against her mouth. "I'm going to take you to bed now."

At that, she took a deep, shaky breath. Her muddled brain unpacked that little announcement, noting that it hadn't been a question, but rather a statement of fact.

Any doctor who has ever worked near an E.R. learns to make quick decisions, even if the consequences may be enormous. In the split second that followed, Callie evaluated the possible repercussions of following Hank into the bedroom. Side effects may include dizziness, loss of dignity and confusion. Not to mention the possibility of another mutually embarrassing incident.

But seriously. Was she really going to take a pass? *Hell no.* And maybe she could get him out of her system.

While her lust-clouded brain did its best to sort through the repercussions, Hank set her on her feet. Before she could wake from her panting stupor, he transferred to his chair in that athletic way he had, like a bad-ass gymnast executing a maneuver from one apparatus to the other. Then he reached for her hands, pulling her down onto his lap. She leaned back on his chest as he steered toward the bedroom. "I've never had a passenger before," he whispered into her ear, before nipping it.

She turned her head to meet his smiling eyes. So he claimed her mouth again, and Callie was only a little surprised when he was able to steer them all the way to the bedside while also burning her up with his kisses.

"We've arrived," he whispered. Then powerful arms scooped her up and tossed her onto the bed, which was a low, modern piece of furniture. Another effortless press of his arms on the chair swung his body over to join her. He used one arm to bring his knees onto the bed, too. And then he gathered Callie up and began covering her neck with kisses. She wrapped her arms around his back, and the volume of all that muscle under her hands made her more than a little giddy.

"You just feel so good," he said into the V-neck of her shirt. "If I promise not to freak out, can I take off some of your clothes?"

She dipped her head to find his lips. His kiss was wet and urgent, but she broke it off to answer him. "Maybe you'd better get naked first, as a guarantee."

His brown eyes smiled up at her. "How about we go shot for shot?"

Callie took a deep breath, giving herself one more chance to come to her senses. But that didn't happen. "Deal," she said instead.

With a grin, he did an ab crunch, stripping his T-shirt to reveal that beautiful chest. For so long, she'd been yearning to reach for him. Now she did, letting her fingers wander down the sunburst tattoo on his pecs. He closed his eyes in appreciation.

When she began to kiss a path across his chest, he made a greedy sound in the back of his throat. "Your turn now," he rumbled, reaching for her shirt buttons. When the shirt fell away, he reached for the strap of her bra.

"Wait," she chided. "I thought we were going shot for shot?"

"Stickler," he whispered. "Have it your way." Then he put his nose between her breasts and licked a line across the border where the bra blocked him from reaching more of her. Her nipples hardened at the very suggestion, and Callie whimpered in spite of herself.

Torturing her further, he placed his mouth over one silk-covered nipple, sucking gently. The warmth of his tongue through the dampened fabric was tantalizing. "Okay, take it off," she begged.

"Rules are rules," Hank chuckled.

"You've never followed a rule in your life," Callie shot back, arching off the bed to get more of her breast into his mouth.

"Good point." Half a second later, he had her bra off and her breast against his tongue. Opening his mouth widely, he sucked her nipple in deep.

"Oh, God yes," Callie hissed. The swirl of his mouth on her aching tip shot a sizzle of longing straight through her core. Just as before, Hank was bringing her from zero to ninety in a hurry. Given their history, it occurred to her that she ought to be more cautious. But everything just felt too good to worry.

With shaking fingers, she reached for his fly, pausing her hand on the button. "Now or never," she whispered.

"Do it," he said. Eager hands reached down to help her. He

shucked off his jeans, leaving his boxer briefs still snug on his waist. Callie reached for the elastic waistband, but he held her hand away. "Not just yet, okay?"

She looked up into his eyes, questioning. But his regarded her warmly. "I'm not chickening out. There's just one more step than there used to be." He kissed her. "Since our disaster at Willow's, I've done some...homework."

Callie grinned up at him, rendered speechless by the image of Hank touching himself.

"Trust me, it's the only kind of homework I was ever good at." He kissed her again, his mouth melting her own. There was plenty of willingness and ambition in that kiss. She didn't object when he liberated her of her own jeans next, leaving her with a pair of silk panties. Then he rolled on top of her, fitting his hips to hers. With kisses that could power the Eastern Seaboard with their intensity, he moved against her. She felt him grow hard against her body, his desire blooming between her legs.

She reached down, skimming her fingers against the bulge in his briefs, stretching her fingers down to rub his sack, and he let out a groan. The way his eyes fell closed as she touched him seemed to indicate that he had pretty good sensation there.

It was hard to shut off thinking like a doctor. Even here.

But then another one of his potent kisses had her shucking off the mental lab coat. "I want to touch you," she whispered.

"I'm all yours now," he said, reaching into his waistband. He eased himself out of the briefs, his hand wrapped around his shaft. Slowly, he massaged his length, and Callie felt herself flush with desire at the sight of him. He was thick and beautiful. She pushed his hands out of the way and took over.

"Hell yes," he said, rolling onto his back. He tugged her

down to kiss him, and so she crawled on top, the silk triangle of her panties meeting his cock.

She stirred her hips, sliding over him until he growled. "You can feel that?" she teased.

"Think so. You'd better do it again just to make sure," he chuckled.

She slid against him, torturing both of them, until he rolled her sideways, grabbed her panties and yanked them down. Even as he continued to kiss her hungrily, his hand slid down between her legs. When his fingers found the pool of moisture waiting there, he moaned into her mouth. "Goddamn, lady." Releasing her he reached over and pulled a condom out of the drawer and dropped it onto the bed.

Callie stopped him. "You can use that if you want to, but…"

He eyed her, fingering the packet. "We don't need this?"

She shook her head. "I'm clean and protected against pregnancy, and you've had every medical test in the book. And I thought…" She cleared her throat. "They diminish sensation."

With a chuckle, he tossed the condom across the room. Then he covered her with his body, his forehead pressing against hers. "Callie, I did something really presumptuous earlier."

"What's that?"

"I took a pill." His lopsided grin was wicked.

"I guess it wasn't an aspirin?"

His dark eyes flashed as he kissed her. "No."

"Something your urologist gave you?"

"Mmm-hmm," he said, his teeth nipping at her lower lip. "And for best results, I need to give it another ten minutes to take effect. I wonder if I can think of a good way to spend the time?" He hitched a bit lower down her body, treating her nipples to more of his worship.

Heat surged between her legs, and she pressed her hips up against him.

"You know," he broke off to slide a bit lower, kissing her belly. "There's one part of me that was never injured."

"What?" she gasped, the weight of him delicious on her body.

"My tongue." He began to kiss his way past her belly button, his lips pausing to close around one hip bone. And then they slid lower, toward the inside of her thigh.

"Oh jeez," she gasped. She felt herself tense up.

He lifted his head. "Not a fan?"

Callie sucked in oxygen. She looked down, stunned at the sight of those gorgeous brown eyes looking up at her from between her legs, and those powerful, inked shoulders hovering between her knees. She flopped her head back against the pillow. "I...I really have no idea if I'm a fan." Nathan had never offered to kiss her there. And whatever drunken exploits she'd undertaken in college were long forgotten.

He made a clucking sound against the inside of her thigh. "Well, then you'll think about it while I taste you. And you can give me your opinion when I'm done."

Callie forced herself to press back against the sheets. At first, his mouth worshipped only the tender skin of her inner leg, and so she relaxed. But while he sucked gently on her thigh, his thumb slid over to trace a lazy circle around her aching bud. She let out her breath in one big gasp. Then, while his thumb wandered down to slick a path around her opening, he moved his lips to the very top edge of her mound, where he dropped gentle kisses that left her quivering with anticipation.

One finger teased its way inside her, and just as she was processing how glorious that felt, his tongue slid slowly onto her clit.

"Oh, my God," she gasped.

His chuckle was muffled by her...*jeez*. But she sucked in another lungful of air and decided to be embarrassed about it later. He backed off for a second while she caught her breath. But then his sneaky fingers crooked deeper inside her, and he lowered his mouth onto her body again. She saw speckles on the insides of her eyelids.

"Oh, sweet Jesus..." she whispered.

"That's right," he said between licks. "Mmm."

She shivered as every nerve ending in her body stood at attention. Her hips rolled toward him—it would have been impossible to keep them still. Hank's mouth picked up a delicious pace, drowning her in sensation. After only a minute or so, she was so close. How was he so good at this? The question stuttered her enjoyment. His nickname said everything, didn't it? He was going to be Hazardous to her heart.

But then he did something that made her forget that pinprick of worry. He closed his lips around her clit and gently sucked.

A cry stuck in her throat as her body suddenly squeezed Hank's fingers. Callie rolled her hips in ecstasy as her climax broke over her, pulsing through her in waves. When she couldn't take it anymore, he gentled his touch. His two thumbs slowly smoothed down her wet mound. Then he placed his lips lightly on her body for one last, tender kiss.

Wrung out, Callie lay still as he crawled back up to lie next to her. He stroked her cheek with the pad of one damp thumb. "I owed you one from that toe curler you gave me on the massage table." He chuckled. "I'm *still* thinking about that day."

She smiled at him, but her heart gave a painful squeeze. For Hank, this was all about gratification—about pounding hearts and curling toes. But Callie knew she would never get this night out of her head, or her heart. Those flashing dark eyes and that lopsided bad-boy smile would forever be burned on her heart. So would the sight of those sculpted shoulders between her thighs.

Nobody else would ever compare. The Nathans of the world would never be enough anymore.

Callie skimmed Hank's exquisite chest with her hands and tried not to care too much.

Hank pulled Callie close, stroking her back while she recovered. She lay sweet and flushed in his arms, and he was enjoying every moment. He hadn't had sex for the better part of a year, and he was bursting for it. But really, what was another ten minutes between friends? Tonight he would get there. And if for some reason it didn't work, he would talk her into trying again tomorrow. He was through with worrying.

And anyway, Callie was a girl to go slow with, to savor. His days of banging a strange girl in the bathroom of a bar were over, and it had taken him almost a year to discover that he didn't actually care. All that time without intimacy—and fearing himself incapable of it—was a surefire way to remember what it was really for. If you did it right, sex was as close as you could be to someone. And here in his bed was the woman he most wanted to be close to. He pressed his face into Callie's hair and breathed deeply.

After a time, she shifted position, reaching her hand down to stroke his cock, which miraculously was still hard. Hank sent out silent prayers of gratitude to whichever big pharmaceutical company was playing wingman tonight.

No fear, he reminded himself. Before last December, Hank had never had any trouble with courage. Failure was his friend. For every trick that Hank had landed in competition, he'd face-planted two dozen times beforehand. And he'd always been cool with that. When he'd found a boundary that his body did not seem to want to cross, he'd only become more determined to make it work.

Until recently.

He'd let his shock and fear take over. And the result was pure disaster. Anxiety hadn't done him any favors. In fact, anxiety had made him act like an ass.

But no more. Hank closed his eyes and sank into the sensation of Callie's touch. Things didn't feel exactly the same as they had before his accident. But now that he wasn't panicking anymore, he was capable of saying that they felt pretty damned good. This new version of arousal was more like a slow burn than a tinderbox. Either way, he was hot for her, and the anticipation had his stomach muscles tightening as her soft hand stroked him.

"Mmm," he said, taking her touches as an invitation. He rolled over, blanketing her body with his own.

"You feel good up there," she breathed.

He kissed her slowly, settling his hips against hers. The air was heavy with anticipation between them. "I want you, Callie. Can I have you?"

She nodded, cupping her hand around the nape of his neck.

It took him a moment to organize his wayward legs

between hers. Then he pressed up on one arm, using his other hand to guide himself toward home. How many times had he done this in his lifetime? He had no idea. All he knew was that he had never once appreciated it as much as he did right now. "Callie..." he whispered as the crown of his cock sank inside. Without a condom, all the wet velvet of her body seemed to drink him in.

Her sexy, hooded eyes held his as he slowly pushed inside. She was so warm and tight that he had to close his eyes and draw another deep breath. She spread her legs to take him all the way in, and he stretched her until he was seated to the hilt against her body.

And then, overwhelmed, he dropped his face into the comfort of her hair.

"Hello, gorgeous," she murmured, one hand stroking the nape of his neck. Then two hands skimmed down his back. He felt her fingertips sweep downward toward the supersensitive band at his waist, and he shivered in her arms. So slowly as to be torturous, she did it again.

God, there was nothing better than this.

With a growl, he reared up to claim her mouth for his own, tasting her and sliding his tongue against hers. He pressed his forearms down on the bed and used his triceps to rock his body back and forth over hers until she began to whimper with gratitude.

"Callie," he rasped. "I don't think I can go slow. The first time is going to be fast and sweaty."

"Do it," she gasped.

"Do what, gorgeous?" He looked into her eyes and smiled. If he could get her to ask him to fuck her again, he would be only too happy to say yes.

But she only narrowed her eyes, then reached a hand down

to slap him on the ass.

With a chuckle, he dropped a quick kiss onto her pouting mouth. "All right, even if you won't ask, I'm still going to make you yell my name." Her eyes went a little wide, and her cheeks flushed pink. God, she was terrific. And she was gorgeous, and he was the lucky bastard buried deep inside her.

Unbelievable.

Hank stretched one arm overhead, grasping the rail of his modern iron headboard. He used the handhold as an anchor, thrusting deeper into her, quickening his pace. Beneath him, Callie's breath came in gasps. He gentled his motion, slowing down. "Too much?"

"No, don't stop," she panted, pressing her hips up against him.

He couldn't help but give a loud groan of happiness. Bending his arm again, he drove into her. Every stroke felt richer than the last. Callie was here in his bed at last, holding him with every part of her body, her sweet breath on his skin, her warmth seeping into his very soul.

There had never been a more perfect moment in his life. All his frustrations fell away, replaced by a potent cocktail of affection and triumph. Every part of him—even the scars he carried on his body and in his heart—came alive for this moment. All his prior suffering was here with him, too, every bit of it feeding and stoking today's pleasure. Until now, he hadn't understood that one made the other so much sweeter.

As he moved, Callie splayed her fingers out against both sides of his torso. Each slide of his body caused her fingertips to drag like rakes onto his sensitive waist. The effect made him shiver. "Harder," he bit out. Her fingertips became fingernails, and he nearly hollered at the thrill of it.

"God, kiss me," she breathed.

He plunged his tongue into her mouth, and she arched off the bed with a moan. Her breaths became gasps. He kept up his end of their excellent bargain, pumping against her beautiful body, kissing her as if his life depended on it. And in a way, it did. Somehow he'd arrived at this point, in spite of his own fear and stubbornness. Callie was handing him his life back, and he didn't even deserve it.

Then she clung to him, crying out with each stroke. And the sound of her pleasure detonated him. He felt his balls tighten and his hips buck, while a furious tingle spread through his pelvis. And then he was pouring himself into a woman for the first time in almost a year. "Oh Jesus," he gasped. "Finally." He clenched again and again before finally collapsing onto his forearms, panting into Callie's neck.

And then all was still; the only sounds were their own quick breaths. Still inside her, he licked a bead of sweat from Callie's collarbone. She put a hand over her face and turned her head. But he lifted it and looked into her eyes. "Still with me, gorgeous?"

Callie smiled, breathing hard. "That was intense."

He touched his lips to hers. "I think we both needed that. Very, very badly." Reluctantly he disengaged, sliding down to her side, gathering his girl into his arms and holding her close. "Callie. There aren't even words for how I feel right now."

In answer, she gave only a happy sigh.

Hank closed his eyes and felt more peace than he had in a very long time.

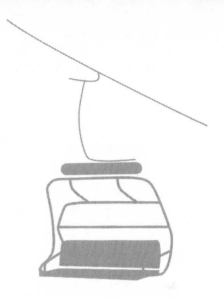

CHAPTER
FIFTEEN

CURLED up in Hank's arms, Callie felt blissed out. Hank traced gentle circles on her back with his fingertips. Eventually, his hand dragged across her waistline, under her belly button. The sensation made her shiver. "Right here," he said, his voice hoarse. His fingers drew a horizontal line across her belly. "It's the weirdest thing. When you touch me here, it makes me crazy. It's almost embarrassing."

She twined her fingers through his. "As a kink, needing to have your waist tickled isn't so outrageous. Not when there are people who use whips and chains. Or shove pieces of fruit into their orifices."

"*Fruit?* Are you shitting me?"

"When you work next door to the E.R. for a couple of years, you see some things."

He laughed, and she snuggled into his body. His fingers stroked a lock of her hair across his chest. "I always wondered how your hair would feel right here," he murmured. "The answer is: awesome."

But Callie had become distracted by thoughts of the hospital. "Hank," she whispered. "This job I applied for in California…"

He moved fast. Before she knew what was happening, he found her lips with his. After a lingering kiss, he said, "Every time you bring that up I'm just going to kiss you again."

She returned the kiss, taking the hint. It wasn't really the time to discuss it, was it? She had just had the best sex of her life, and the important conversations could just wait a few more hours.

Outside Hank's window, the sky had blackened, and they were still wrapped in the wonderful cocoon of one another. She enjoyed the feel of his lips grazing her brow line, and the rock-hard muscles of his painted chest. But then, even through the fog of post-coital bliss, Callie was sure she heard footsteps on the other side of the bedroom door. "Um, Hank…?"

He shifted quickly, yanking the comforter up over the two of them. Callie froze as she heard a quick knock, followed by a man's voice. "Hazardous? Are you in there?"

Hank lifted his head to answer. "Give us a few minutes, man."

"Christ!" an oddly familiar voice said. "Typical Hazardous." She heard a chuckle move away from the door again.

"What the hell?" Callie whispered. "Are you having guests, Hank? Why didn't you say anything?"

He wiggled his eyebrows. "Because I was trying to get you into my bed, Callie. What fool would mention company?"

She didn't know whether to laugh or cry. "This is going to be awkward. Is there a back door I can sneak out of?"

"Don't you dare," he chuckled. "We're all friends here."

She looked around his shoulder again, toward the door. But it was shut. "How do you figure?"

Hank leaned down, touching his forehead to hers. "You know who that was, right?"

She shook her head.

"That was Dane. They're staying with me."

"What?" She wiggled out from under him, sitting up. "Willow is here, too? How do I not know this? Oh…" She palmed her forehead. "There was a voice mail and three texts."

Hank gave a belly laugh. "The good doctor is behind on her messages."

"I've been a little preoccupied."

"With what?" He lifted his head and sucked her nipple into his mouth.

"Oh, my God," Callie fell back onto the pillows. "Please stop. I can't think when you do that."

"Thinking is overrated." He gave her other breast some of the same before sitting up. "But I guess it would be rude if I didn't greet our guests. Though I bet Dane has already found the beer."

Callie put her face in her hands. "Can I jump in your shower for a minute? Or, like, three hours? That's how long it will take to compose myself."

He wrapped his arms around her waist. "Only if you promise to stay here tonight. I'm not ready to let you go."

Hank waited until he heard the shower running before wriggling into his jeans. Once dressed, he wheeled into the living room. "Sorry about that."

Dane grinned at him from over the rim of a can of Heady Topper. "Don't apologize, man. I should have known better than to go around knocking on doors. I forgot who I was dealing with."

"No kidding." Hank couldn't resist adding this bit of bravado, even though Dane could have wandered through his bedroom every day for the past eleven months without finding anyone inside other than his lonely ass. "Hey, Dane? Be cool to her, okay? It's a new thing."

"When am I not cool?" Dane winked.

Willow came in the front door then, carrying a very sleepy toddler. "She didn't want to wake up. Hi, Hazardous!" She ran over and planted a kiss on his cheek. Then she looked around. "Where's Callie? I saw her car in the driveway."

At that, Dane choked on his beer.

"Are you okay?" Willow trotted over to pat her man on the back, but he began to grin even as he sputtered.

"Callie?" Dane coughed.

Hank shook his head. "I told you to be cool, dude."

Dane threw back his head and laughed. "It's always the quiet ones."

"What's so funny?" Willow demanded. "Where's Callie?"

"You might check the bedroom," Dane grinned, pointing with his beer can.

Willow's eyes grew wide with understanding. Without a word, she handed the little girl to Dane, who took Finley in one arm. Then she headed for the bedroom door. "Callie?" she said, knocking twice. Then she opened the door and disappeared behind it.

When Callie came out of Hank's bathroom, Willow was sitting on the corner of the bed, just a few feet from the scene of the crime. "Callie," she said. "Last time we spoke I asked you 'what's up,' and you said 'nothing.' You're not a shoo-in for Best Friend of the Year if you leave the good stuff out." Callie could tell she was fighting off a smile.

"In my defense," Callie said, straightening her shower-dampened hair, "there wasn't any good stuff to tell when we last spoke."

"That's no excuse," Willow grinned. "At least I know why you were too busy to return my messages. I'm not even offended. So... you and Hank are an item. I didn't see that coming."

"I wouldn't call us an item." Callie felt her cheeks heat. "It's casual."

For a second, her friend said nothing. "I've gotta throw a flag on that statement. Nothing you do is casual, Callie."

That didn't sound fair. "Maybe I don't want to be that boring girl anymore."

"Hey! I didn't say you were boring." Willow laid a hand on Callie's elbow. "You're smart. You're thoughtful. And you're loyal. So if you're trying to tell me that Hank is just a fuck buddy, I'll have trouble believing it."

Callie straightened her T-shirt and tried to think. "I like Hank a lot," she admitted. "But there hasn't been any discussion of a relationship yet." And why would there be? "He's still putting his life together. It isn't the right moment to pressure him to commit. Besides, you told me yourself that he's a party animal. And not exactly a relationship guy."

Willow winced. "He had one relationship, right?"

"After the way it ended, why would he be looking for another?"

Her friend threw her hands in the air. "Callie, you won't know unless you ask."

"True," Callie admitted. But great sex did not a relationship make. And it didn't even seem fair to start asking questions. "Hey, where's Finley?"

"I handed her off to Dane."

Callie put a hand on the bedroom doorknob. "Dane isn't going to let me live this down, is he?"

"Nope!" Willow said cheerfully. "So you might as well face the music."

Hank had stoked the fire and stirred the chili. Then he'd brought Dane another beer, and transferred to the other end of the sofa. The baby reclined in Dane's lap as if her father were a chaise lounge. She drank her own beverage of choice out of a bottle, while her big moony eyes tipped upward, watching Dane, listening to his voice through the vibrations in his chest.

The comfortable way his friend's hand rested on her chubby leg was hard to look at, somehow. The guys on the circuit used to mourn for every one of their cohort who got married and settled down. But Dane looked as happy as Hank had ever seen him.

Hank distracted himself by propping both legs onto the coffee table, stretching out his quadriceps. His leg muscles had begun to spasm. The reflex was almost certainly caused by all the action in bed earlier.

It had been totally worth it.

"I hope Willow can convince Callie to come out here," Hank chuckled, tipping his head toward the bedroom door.

Dane grinned. "But how will they talk about you, then?"

"Good point." Hank took a swig of his beer and refused to worry about it.

The bedroom door opened and both women came out.

"Oh, my God, she's huge!" Callie exclaimed, running toward Finley. She sat down on the big sofa between Hank and Dane, and gave baby Finley's little foot a squeeze.

Dane held up a hand to Callie for a high five. "Good to see you," he said. And after she smacked it, he added "…with your clothes on."

"*Dane*," she warned as he laughed.

Hank leaned forward, putting his hands on Callie's hips and hauling her backward across the expanse of leather until she was close to him. "Don't listen to him," he said, sliding an arm around her waist.

"I try not to," she said, her voice dipping. He wanted her to turn around, to give him a smile. But she didn't.

"Who needs another drink?" Willow asked.

"Callie needs a new snakebite," Hank said. "I brought her a drink earlier, and then didn't let her drink it."

"*Hank*," she whispered.

"Sorry." But he wasn't, not really. She made him want to beat on his chest in victory. The sexy, intelligent woman in his arms was finally his girl. He'd almost wrecked their chance to be together. Gently, Hank reached around to cup her chin and turn her face toward him. When he found Callie's eyes, there was a quiver of uncertainty in them. "Hey, are you okay?"

"Sure," she said, her gaze sliding away.

Hank lifted one of her hands, giving her palm a brief kiss. If she was feeling skittish about everything that went down between them tonight, that was understandable. Maybe he could get a quiet moment alone with her later. Given the chance, he'd tell her a dozen times tonight how much it meant to him to have her there.

Willow fetched a beer for Callie and a soda for herself, then took a seat on the opposite end of the L-shaped sectional, which meant that four—no *five*—friends occupied his giant sectional sofa. It had been a long time since his lonely little house had held so many contented faces. Hank took another drink and felt lucky for the tenth time in an hour.

Outside, there was the sound of gravel kicked up by car tires. Willow carried her soda over to the window and looked out. "You have a guest. Two cars, actually."

"That's probably Bear," Hank said. "I told him you guys were here tonight. And maybe my sister? I left her a message earlier."

A quick series of footsteps could be heard on the ramp outside. "Hey, guys!" Bear stepped inside, his eyes finding Hank's. "I hope you don't mind that I brought the star of my commercial," he said quickly. "She's staying with me."

"You cannot be serious," Hank spat.

Bear looked guilty. "I should have called ahead."

"Too late now," Hank grumbled.

Callie watched, helpless, as Hank's ex-girlfriend swept inside. Heedless of the pile of shoes near the door, Alexis stalked across the wood floors in her high-heeled boots. "Hi all!" She stopped in front of Hank, leaning over to give him a quick kiss. On the *lips*. Callie felt a flash of irritation, but then the Skier Barbie moved on. "Dane, what a cute baby!" she cried.

"How are you, Alexis?" Dane said. Since they were both on the U.S. ski team, of course they knew each other. Though Callie couldn't help but notice that Dane's greeting lacked a certain amount of enthusiasm.

"I'm great! My God, Hank. I *love* the renovation." She sashayed into kitchen. "I'll bet we can still make a decent margarita in here. For old times' sake."

She looked very, very comfortable in Hank's space, and

Callie felt a little smaller with every passing second. In Hank's kitchen, Alexis cut a lime in half and began to squeeze the juice into a blender. "You do have tequila, right?" she asked with a toss of her hair. "You always have tequila."

Ugh. Callie knew she shouldn't be thinking jealous thoughts about Hank. She didn't have any claims on him. All the same, she didn't need to watch his ex marking her (former) territory. "Hey, Willow?" Callie asked. "Didn't you say you wanted to swing by and say hello to Travis? I'll drive you into town."

"But I was just about to break out the chili," Hank said.

"I'll do it," Alexis volunteered, reaching for the stack of bowls on the counter.

Callie gave her best friend the laser beam eyes. *Help me, here,* she silently begged.

Willow cocked her head to study Callie before she spoke. "Well, sure. Let's swing by Rupert's. And if we miss dinner, we'll get Travis to bring us a bite to eat." Rising from the sofa, she leaned over Dane and the baby. Before lifting Finley, Willow ran her fingers through the hair on the back of Dane's head in a gesture so intimate and familiar that it made Callie's heart ache. "We're going to show off the baby. Back in an hour or so?"

He gave her a kiss and handed Finley up to her.

"Spill," Willow demanded from the passenger seat of Callie's car. "Why did you want to get out of there so badly? The two of you look cute together, and Hank is such a hottie."

"That he is."

"And that sexy voice...wow." Willow giggled. "Just give your married friend *one* detail. Don't make me beg."

Callie felt her face heat. "Like what? It isn't nice to kiss and tell."

"I dunno. Just one teeny, tiny thing," Willow begged.

"Fine—he definitely does not have a teeny, tiny thing."

Willow giggled. "I'm so happy for you both. It sounds terrible to say, but I'm glad to hear that he can..." She cleared her throat.

"You're not nearly as glad as he is," Callie quipped. But that was all she would ever say on the matter. No one needed to know how anxious the question had made him, or how distraught they'd both been.

"You two look great together," Willow said.

"Seriously? I'll bet he looked pretty good with Sporty Barbie back in the day."

Willow snorted. "Hank did *not* look happy to see her. He looked pissed. What's Alexis doing in town, anyway? She trains in Utah. But I think she grew up near Stowe."

Callie shrugged, miserable. "She was shooting a commercial today. For the Vermont Tourist Board, or something like that. And she's here to look blonde and fancy in comparison to me."

"Callie! Stop."

"I know I'm being morose. But on top of all the other complications, I know I'm not really Hank's type."

"How can you be so sure? He seems really into you. I'm serious."

"He... I know he was quite the player." A few weeks ago, Callie had broken down and searched Hank's exploits on the internet. She'd learned that he and Alexis were an item for less than one year. Before that, there were *People* magazine pictures of him with a dozen other models and female athletes. "I just feel like there's an expiration date on his heart, and I'm going to be left behind. I was thinking of taking preventative measures."

"Is there such a thing as a vaccine against broken hearts?"

"Willow, I'm still going to apply for that job in Marin. They won't interview me until January, anyway. Besides, I like the idea of being closer to you guys. Like, a cheap-flight-for-the-weekend distance."

"But...hang on a second. You've been making noises about leaving Vermont, because you haven't met a guy. But now you've met a guy that you really like...and you want to leave, so he won't break your heart? Why wouldn't you give it a fair chance, first? If it ends badly, move wherever you want."

"Did you see his ex? She's an Olympian and a model. I'm never going to be able to compete with that."

"But I'm not those things, and I'm married to one."

"You're beautiful and perfect. And you make pastry from scratch."

"Callie, God. If you don't love him, then go. But if you think you might, then don't. You're being a chicken. He's *not* out of your league."

Crap. Willow's logic was giving her a headache. "It doesn't matter, because I can't have him, anyway. We work too closely at the hospital. I'm not his doctor, but people won't give me the benefit of the doubt. It would look so inappropriate on paper. He got me the job as the study researcher."

"That sounds like an excuse," Willow grumbled.

"It isn't, I swear." Tonight she'd put her reputation on the line, and all because Hank had made her feel sexy. She was supposed to be smarter than that. Yet she'd made the same mistake again. Something about being in the same room with that man lowered her IQ by an easy twenty points. "Willow, I know I can't have Hank if I move to California. But I can't really have him if I stay here, either. I'm not just chickening out."

"Nobody knows chickens like I do, Callie," Willow quipped. She used to raise them. "And I'm sitting next to one right now."

"Not true."

"Bawk, bawk, bawk!"

"Stop."

CHAPTER
SIXTEEN

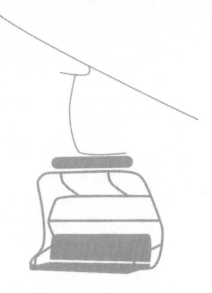

LATER, when Alexis got up to go to the bathroom, Hank gave Bear a look. "Dude, why? Why did you bring her here? She chased my girl away."

"Sorry, Hazardous. I didn't know you had a girl. And I just thought it would do you good to see this one again, and realize you didn't lose out on anything. Also, she's killing me, and I needed backup. There's only so much Alexis a guy can take."

Hank frowned into his empty bottle. Bear was right, of course. It's just that Hank didn't need the reminder anymore.

"I'm leaving this folder right here." Bear pointed at the coffee table. "Promise me you'll read it tomorrow."

"Should I assume this is about your film?"

"Yep. Read it. And pay special attention to the itinerary. Because I want to buy your plane tickets, like, this month."

Hank snorted. "You can buy all the tickets you want, but that doesn't mean I'm getting on the plane."

"Yes you are. I'm even going to let you drive the snowcat when we go to Sun Valley. Somebody has to."

That idea silenced Hank, because Bear made him picture it —the pre-dawn sky, the sleepy riders queuing up to climb into the heavy vehicle. The crunch of snow under boots, and the puffs their breath would make as they swung aboard, thermoses of coffee in hand. The smack talk. He felt a powerful pull to be part of that again.

Shit. He sneaked a look at Bear, who was sitting back, hands behind his head, looking pleased with himself.

Dane brought another round of beers over to the sofa.

"Dude," Bear said to him. "Your baby is so cute. I don't even like babies."

Dane grinned. "Guys keep asking me how I've survived with a kid. But two years ago I was the loneliest asshole there was. Now I have a pretty girl in my bed every night, and a child who thinks I walk on water."

"You don't have to sell it to me," Hank said in a low voice. "This place echoes."

"Well, Hazardous, you can get carpets or a girl," Bear said. "Or go big and get both."

Dane put down his beer bottle. "Speaking of going big, I brought some Cubans. Who wants a cigar?"

"Hell yes," Hank said. "But let's smoke them out on the deck so we don't stink the place up."

"He's getting all domesticated," Bear said. "Next thing you know he'll be asking us to put our beer in a glass."

"As long as there's beer, what difference would it make? I'm just going to grab a sweatshirt." He rolled into his bedroom and found the condom on top of the laundry basket in front of his dresser. He jammed it into his pocket with a smile, then opened his dresser drawer.

"What's so funny?" Alexis was just coming out of his bathroom, pressing her lips together in that way women do after reapplying their makeup.

"Nothing." He let the sweatshirt fall into his lap instead of putting it on. She was the last person he wanted to see him struggle, even with something as stupid as pulling on a shirt. He wanted to roll out the door again, but she sat down on the bed beside him, as if to strike up a conversation. *Damn.* "How've you been, Hazardous?" She twirled a bit of her hair around one finger.

"Good, really good." And damn if it wasn't the truth. Now, if Alexis would just get the fuck out, he would be even better. Not only had she scared Callie off, but she was keeping him from a Cuban cigar.

But instead of leaving, Alexis put her hands up to cup his face. "I'm so glad to hear it. You sure *look* good."

He held very, very still, wondering how best to extract himself from this conversation.

"We had some good times, didn't we?" She slid forward toward him and planted a soft kiss on his lips. "We had some hot times."

He eased back in his chair, buying himself a few crucial inches. "Alexis…"

Her hands strayed from his face down his chest. Fuck, she wasn't going there, was she? Her fingers dipped lower, and he caught them as they began to approach his belly button. Only Alexis would actually go there.

And *he* was the one they called Hazardous?

"How about one more, for old time's sake?" She smiled, her blue eyes flashing. That smile used to drive him wild, but now it just looked a bit manic. "Come on, Hazardous? When was the last time you had sex?" She patted his fly. "It still works, right?"

No longer interested in saving her feelings, he wheeled himself back about a foot, to give himself some space. "Alexis, seriously? You'd cheat on your man, just to throw me a mercy fuck?"

Her smile wavered. "You don't have to be rude."

"And you don't have to be..." *such a crazy bitch.* He took a deep breath. "There's something going on with you, isn't there? Don't take this the wrong way, Alexis, but you're acting kind of crazy." *Even for you,* he might have added.

She dropped her head but didn't say anything.

"Did you break up with him or something?" No—that wasn't it. Something clicked for Hank, and he had a sudden hunch about his ex-girlfriend's ridiculous behavior. "You're freaking out about getting married, aren't you? When is the date, a month from now?"

She pushed her yellow hair off her face. "Is it that obvious?" she whispered.

"Aw, buddy," Hank chuckled, giving her arm a single squeeze. "You can't use me to exorcise your demons." *Not anymore, anyway.* "That is so rude."

"I know," she sighed. "Sorry." She was quiet for a moment. "I'm not sure if I'm going to go through with it."

Ouch. Hank did not know what to say. She was so young. Just twenty-five years old, and anything at all seemed possible. Life hadn't handed her any real setbacks yet. It was both an envious and a torturous position, wasn't it? Because she was just beginning to understand that choices had the power to alter the shape of your life.

Hank knew that already. Maybe he learned it the hard way, but he'd learned it all the same. And that meant that the next wonderful choice that came along wouldn't scare the shit out of him like it was doing to Alexis.

And now he knew what to say. "Next time you're in the same room with him, ask your gut what to do. It will tell you."

She raised her eyes. "I hope so."

"You'll be okay," he said, patting her hand.

She caught it in hers and squeezed. "You do look good, Hank. Seriously."

"Thank you," he said. *And thank you for extinguishing any final regrets I may have harbored.* "But I think it's time for you to leave."

She gave him a catty little smile. "Your loss." She stood up then, and turned her back on him, heading for the living room.

He followed her out. As she reached the front door, he said, "And not that it's any of your business. But the answer to your question is—an hour or two ago."

She chuckled as she went for the door. "Glad to hear it," she said over her shoulder. And then she was gone.

"What happened there?" Dane asked as the door closed.

Hank pulled his sweatshirt over his head. "I had to get rid of her so we could smoke a cigar in peace. Now, let's get to it, before the women come back." He rolled toward the door.

Outside on the porch, his friends reclined on the deck chairs. Dane trimmed the ends, and Hank chain-lit the stogies. Their burning orange tips were the only light on the porch. Hank put the cigar in his mouth and gave several quick puffs to assure his light. "God, Alexis is such a piece of work. She just propositioned me."

Bear's eyebrows shot up, and he began to choke.

"Do we need to put training wheels on that thing for you?" Dane asked.

"I don't even know what's worse. The fact that she put the moves on me, or the fact that she asked me—and this is a quote—if 'it still works.'"

"*Christ,*" Dane swore.

"I mean, it's a fair question," Hank acknowledged. "But only the very rude are willing to ask. I should get T-shirts made."

He enjoyed the sound of his friends' laughter in the dark. "Of course it still works," Bear said. "Hazardous is a force of nature."

Hank couldn't even answer. Tonight, at long last, he was filled with the realization of just how lucky he really was. Nothing in this life was a given. There were guys out there who had lost so much more—guys just like him. If he'd hit the pipe's edge harder, he might have no feeling below his belly button. And if he'd landed just ten inches higher up on his spine, he might need a nurse to hold his cigar. There was no logic, and no justice, but he'd been spared.

He was lucky, goddamn it. Only he hadn't felt lucky for a long time. He was so fucking lucky, and he needed to never forget that again. His eyes burned, either from the cigar smoke, or all the emotions in his sappy head. And what did it matter? He was alive, and sitting on the porch with a fine cigar and even finer friends.

In the distance, the sky glimmered with the promise of a bright moon soon to rise in front of the Green Mountains. Hank puffed smoke out of his mouth and watched for it, more content than he'd been for a very long time.

Finley fell asleep on the way back from her first trip to Rupert's Bar.

For a happy hour, Callie had forgotten her troubles. It was just like old times, sitting next to Willow on a bar stool, sharing a plate of nachos. The only difference was watching Travis trying to tap beers holding a toddler on one hip.

Now the little cutie was sacked out in her car seat. "Will she wake up when you lift her out of the backseat?" Callie asked.

"Nope," Willow answered. "She's a good sleeper now. But I hope Dane set up the portable crib while we were gone. What are the odds?"

"If all the beer ran out, then I give you fifty percent."

Willow giggled.

"You seem happy, Wills. All three of you do."

"I *am* happy. But it's work, of course. The baby takes a lot out of us sometimes. It's getting better now that she's turned one."

"Do you think you'll have another one?"

"Actually…I'm pregnant."

Callie was so surprised she might have driven the car off the road. "What?"

"Yeah. Just ten weeks, though. We aren't really telling people."

"Oh, my God, Willow! You're going to have *two* of them. Congratulations."

"We decided that having them close together would be nice. Dane said—and I'm not kidding—that it would be better to get everyone on skis quicker."

Callie howled with laughter. "And did you have a say in it?"

"Of course I did. It's actually better for my career this way. Once I'm ready to open my own psych practice, there will be no way to take a maternity leave."

"Wow. Just…wow." There was silence in the car as Callie turned off the main road and onto the twisting lane that led to

Hank's house. "You know, I could have used a little psych consult around here lately."

"Yeah? Is Hank doing okay?"

"He's had a tough time. I think he's just starting to do better. But I think it's unfair of me to expect things from him. It hasn't even been a year since his accident. I mean…I want to have kids someday, too. How can you ask a guy to think about those big questions, when his whole world has just landed on its ass?"

"It's tough, honey. You can only listen to your gut. If you truly want to go to California, then go. But make sure you're doing it for the right reasons."

Callie sighed. "I'm *so* confused."

"I know, sweetie. That's because you want something, but you're afraid to take it."

"Sure. But there are very good reasons to be afraid. The worst-case scenario is that I could lose my job, *and* Hank and it wouldn't work out. Then I'd have exactly nothing. I'll be asking people whether or not they want fries with their burgers for a living. And I'll live alone with a dozen cats, all of whom have to eat whichever cat food is on sale at the Quick Mart."

"Whoa, there. That's a whole lot of doom. One problem at a time, okay? How can you figure out if the hospital would object to your relationship with Hank?"

"I could ask the director," Callie said immediately. "But since I've already…" She cleared her throat. "The time to ask has long since passed. I'm already guilty."

"So it's not an easy conversation."

"Hell no."

"But is Hank worth a difficult conversation?"

Ouch. "Jeez, if you put it like that…"

"Well, is he?"

Callie put on her right-turn signal and pulled onto the shoulder. She dug her phone out of her pocket and turned it on.

"Dare I ask what you're doing?"

"Having a difficult conversation with the hospital director." She pulled up Dr. Fennigan's number. But then the phone was swept from her hand. "Hey!"

"Callie. Do you know it's eleven o'clock on a Sunday night?"

"Oh." Callie put her head down on the steering wheel. "I'm losing my mind, Willow."

"A little bit."

"He makes me crazy. And stupid."

"That's not always a bad thing."

"I'm not used to feeling stupid."

"Or crazy," Willow added. "But all the best things in life make you feel that way. Roller coasters. Margaritas. Hot sex. Did Nathan ever make you feel crazy like that?"

"No. Of course not."

"Aha! Another clue that Hank matters."

"Get out of my brain, Willow. This is too much truth for one night."

"Just be thankful you get the best-friend discount. Because that was two hundred bucks worth of therapy right there. Now let's get back, shall we?"

With a sigh, Callie put her signal on and checked the country road for traffic. There wasn't any.

Beside her, Willow smiled in the dark. "I know you're scared. But I have a good feeling about this. I probably don't know Hank as well as you do. But he's so *alive*, Callie. And you can't have love without risk, no matter who it is."

"I *know* that. But there's risk, and then there's Hank. I think he invented the word." Callie accelerated toward Hank's house.

"Nathan looked like a sure bet. And look how that turned out."

"Now, that's just mean."

"No it isn't. I'm just pointing out how hard it is to tell who makes a good risk."

"Noted." Callie was now officially exhausted. When she rolled the car up Hank's driveway, she wondered how best to make her exit. Hank wasn't going to like it. But there were tricky conversations to be had with herself, and also with Hank. And she didn't want to muddy their happy party with her fears.

Unfortunately, her thoughts of a quick getaway were dashed when Willow asked her to hold baby Finley. "Setting up the portable crib is a two-man job," she said. "Dane and I will hustle with it, if you wouldn't mind sitting with her."

So Callie got out of the car and accepted a warm bundle from Willow, tucking Finley's soft little head against her shoulder. "Come here, sweetie," she whispered as the little girl's heavy body slumped against hers. Willow removed the car seat from the back of Callie's sedan, and together they crunched up the gravel walk.

"Hark, who goes there?" said a slightly drunk voice. There were three little orange lights on the porch as they approached.

"It's the authorities," Willow quipped. "Hide the booze and the hookers."

Callie, with precious cargo in her arms, took care on the steps in the dark.

"Dane," Willow asked, standing over her husband. "Give

Callie your seat, would you? I need your help with the crib thingy."

Dane stood up to follow his wife inside. And then Bear declared that it was late. He scooped up a few bottles and carried them into the house.

Callie and Hank were alone on the porch together. She reclined against the porch chair, with Finley sleeping on her chest.

"What do you have there?" he asked, his voice low.

An angel, Callie almost answered. For her, it was such a loaded question. The pull she felt toward Hank was intense. But he wasn't a family guy, and she wasn't getting any younger. In her arms, Callie felt as if she was holding a warm bundle of her possible future. Only time would tell if she was lucky enough to have one of these of her own. "Finley fell asleep in the car," Callie said.

"I've never had a baby as a house guest before," he said. "Then again, I don't get many guests."

"They don't take up much space," Callie said. But it wasn't even true. Children occupied a big space in people's lives, and a giant chunk of her heart.

"I've got nothing but space." He sounded as melancholy as Callie felt, and she wondered what had made him sad. Hank stabbed out his cigar in the dark. He took a long pull of beer, and then wheeled around the table toward her. "Move over, gorgeous," he said.

Callie hesitated. Then she made a little space on the lounge chair, and he swung his butt onto it. His arm came around, over her shoulders, and she and Finley were gathered close to his chest. And it was really too much. Sitting like this with him, holding the warmth of a baby's body—it made her ache for everything in life that she might never find.

Hank turned his head, nosing into her hair. The kiss that landed on her temple was a tender one. "Thank you for putting me back in the saddle, you sexy thing," he said.

The sentiment made her heart twist. He was still thinking about sex, and she was weighed down with big questions. Anything she said in reply was going to come out wrong.

Fortunately, that was when Willow opened the door. "All set," she said. "I'll take her."

Callie lurched to her feet and stepped just inside Hank's house. She didn't remove her shoes, as she wasn't planning to stay. "Good night, Finley," she whispered. Handing the baby back to Willow, she could still feel the warm place on her body where the baby had lain.

"I should turn in," Willow said. Then she turned to Callie, giving her a pointed stare. To Hank, who was just wheeling into the room, she said, "Thanks for everything."

"Any time," he said. "I love having visitors. Hey—hang on a second, Willow. There's something I need to show you." Hank propelled himself over to a bookshelf on the wall. And when he turned around, Callie saw Willow's violin case on his lap.

"Where'd you get that?" Willow asked.

"Your house," he said, glancing toward Callie. "It's kind of a long story…"

Callie gave him her best wry smile.

"…But when I saw it, I had a hunch about this fiddle. And I was right." He flipped open the snap lock on the case and opened the lid. "I had the instrument and the bow restrung for you, and the bridge adjusted." Tossing the case onto the coffee table, he put the fiddle under his chin.

Then, as Willow's jaw lowered in surprise, he put the bow on the strings and pulled. Callie got goose bumps as a note rose, shimmering, into the stillness of the room. Strains of a slow, lilting fiddle tune rose up into the night. He kept the volume low, but the speed of his fingers and the confident jump of the bow on the strings were captivating. The music washed over her like a bittersweet spell. Hank was beautiful in so many ways. She hoped he knew that.

Drawn by the music, Dane stuck his head out of the guest room and Bear emerged from the bathroom. The looks on their faces were just as Callie pictured her own—sheer awe.

When Hank finished, he let the last note trail out long. And then there was nothing but silence for a moment.

"Damn," Dane said.

"Wow," Callie sighed.

"I need that in my movie…" Bear put in.

"That was *beautiful*," Willow squealed.

"She sounds good, doesn't she?" Hank agreed, turning the fiddle over in his hands. "When I saw this woodworking, I had a feeling I was holding something special. This one was made in the Smoky Mountains in the nineteenth century. Willow, this thing is worth ten or fifteen thousand dollars."

Willow clapped a hand to her cheek. "God! To think it was just sitting there in the empty house. And there were so many months when I was behind on my electric bill. I could have sold it." Hank clicked the violin case shut and held it out to Willow. But Willow shook her head. "It's no use to me right now. I can't *play* it, that's for sure."

"I could sell it for you," Hank offered.

"Why don't you hang on to it for a while, instead?" Willow suggested. "It suits you."

He ran one hand over the case. "I've enjoyed getting to know it."

Willow yawned. "Right now, I need to get to know a bed." She turned toward Dane, who held out his arms to his family.

"G'night guys," Bear said. He zipped his jacket. On his way past Callie, he gave her elbow a friendly squeeze. Then he was gone, the door shut behind him.

She and Hank were the only ones left in the room. "Come to bed," Hank said slowly, as if he already knew she would argue.

"I can't. I'm sorry." She swallowed hard.

"Like hell you can't. We had a big day, Callie. Don't run off."

"We did. We had…really good sex. The best of my life."

"Damn. I hear a 'but' coming on," he whispered.

"But I don't know what happens next. Now that you're in business again, the women of America will take you back with open arms."

His brow furrowed. "Callie, I don't know why you're bugging out on me. Hell yes, I'm happy to have sex again. That's the truth. I'm happy, because it means I get to be with you in a way that isn't compromised and sad. There isn't anyone I want in my bed except for you."

Her heart gave another squeeze. Hank was a good guy, and she knew he was sincere. But also shortsighted. "I have to go home now."

"Why?"

"Because staying will just confuse me."

"You're still talking about going to California."

She nodded.

"Callie, don't leave tonight. If there's some dream job for you in California, I'll have to understand. But you haven't even interviewed for it yet. So there's really no reason why we can't be together right now."

Oh, but there was. There were several dozen reasons. And yet she was probably too muddled at the moment to explain so that he would understand. "I'm in over my head with you. I just need to be in my own space."

His chin dropped. "You said you'd stay."

It was true. She had. Except that she'd been naked at the time. Every time Hank touched her, she lost her mind a little bit, doing things and saying things that weren't in her best interest.

Even now, he put his hands on the wheels of his chair, as if to come closer. So Callie took evasive measures, putting her hand on the doorknob. "Hank, I need to sort myself out, okay? We'll talk tomorrow."

His frown was deep. "Now would be better than tomorrow."

He rolled forward, but Callie opened the door and stepped outside. It was cowardly, but she did it anyway. Turning toward the stoop, she allowed herself one last look at Hank's face. And that was a mistake. The frustration she saw there cut her. He'd stopped on the threshold of the porch. There was no wheelchair ramp here, so when she went out the front, he couldn't even follow her. Even so, his hands were tight on the armrests, as if he were about to defy physics and follow her down the driveway.

But he couldn't.

It felt cruel to march down those steps, where he couldn't follow. But she did it anyway. And then she got into her car and drove away.

The trouble with being a (mostly) good girl was that you could never quite let yourself off the hook.

After a few hours of sleep, Callie awoke at four in the morning, well aware that she'd now committed *two* sins. The first was having sex with Hank before she'd sorted through the ethical complications. The second was dashing off afterward with all the subtlety of Wile E. Coyote's Road Runner.

She'd already risked everything, really. She could lose her entire livelihood if someone wanted to call her on it. And then she had run away before waiting to learn if her big risk had meant anything to Hank.

But did *he* even know? The problem was that it wasn't fair to ask Hank for more than he'd already given. Tiny had put a very sharp point on what a tough position Hank was in. Less than one year out from his accident, he was still trying to figure out what to do with his new life. It just wasn't right to pressure him.

Also, she wasn't sure if she could stand hearing his answer.

Callie gave up on sleep sometime around six. She went in to work early, spending a couple of hours logging study files into her database. All the hard work of setting up the FES study was finished now. For another ten months there would be data to log. And at the end, the results would be analyzed. If she left Vermont, another physician could take over the project with relative ease.

How depressing.

When she was through with every conceivable bit of busy-work, thoughts of Hank took over again. Wondering if he'd called, she dug inside her bag for her phone.

It wasn't there.

Great. She'd left it at Hank's place. She still had no idea what to say to him, or what to ask of him. And yet she'd have to get her phone back.

What to do?

In medical research, it was impossible to search for answers before you'd accurately framed the question. But in this case, there were too many questions. Did Hank want her now? *Probably.* Would he still want her in a year? *Doubtful.* Should she try for a relationship with someone who didn't want to be a family man? *Probably not.* Would she lose her job if she stuck around to find out? *No idea.*

Most of those thorny questions were between her and Hank. But that last one could be solved by someone else. Sweaty with trepidation, Callie called Dr. Fennigan's assistant to ask for a few minutes of the director's time.

"She's traveling to a conference," the young woman replied. "Can I put you down for a meeting next week?"

Next week? Callie's stomach dropped. "Okay. Thank you."

After scribbling down the meeting time, Callie hung up and went to find coffee.

CHAPTER
SEVENTEEN

HANK WOKE up to the sound of people in his kitchen. He listened for a moment to the muffled tones of Willow's voice talking to her child, and wondered what it would be like to wake to sounds of his own family in the next room.

Good luck with that. His bed was empty. And if the frightened look on Callie's face last night was any indication, it might stay that way. As he opened his eyes, his head gave a little throb of disappointment.

Or maybe that was just the effect of cigar smoke and too many beers.

Hank got up, dressed and went out to greet his guests.

"I found the coffee," Dane said immediately.

"Awesome." Hank went over to pour himself a cup. "When is your closing?" he asked.

"We're supposed to be at the lawyer's office at two," Willow said from the dining table, where she was seated with the baby on her lap. "But Dane's trying to get the bank and the buyer to come in earlier."

"Why?" Hank asked, pouring the milk.

"Dude, you didn't hear? It's going to dump. We're trying to get an earlier flight out of Boston if we can."

Hank looked out the window to find the sky a dull gray. So it was going to snow.

"You're getting twelve inches. Pretty good for the second week of November. I'm going to get dressed." Dane shuffled out of the room, mug in hand.

Funny, Hank thought. He hadn't looked at a weather report in months. Every other year of his life, he would have begun staring at the forecast weeks ago, hoping to see the snowflake icon on the screen, making bets with his buddies. Now there would be snowflakes falling past his window again, and he had no idea how to feel about it.

There were two ways to go, really. Bear wanted him to get outside again and help him to write a film about snowboarders. That would be interesting, but it would come with a constant ache. A bad one. The other choice was to learn to ignore the snow. If he was successful, it would become the same nuisance to him as it was to those who'd never strapped their feet onto a board and flown downhill.

Which was it going to be? Hank's eye was drawn to the folder that Bear had left on the table. It wouldn't hurt to look it over.

"Is Callie going to get out of bed, or what?" Willow asked, putting a few Cheerios down on the table for the baby to grab.

"You'll have to call her to ask."

Willow looked up suddenly, surprise on her face. "Really? She's not here?"

He gave his head a single shake.

"That dope," Willow muttered.

Hank was inclined to agree. Because the alternative was thinking that she just didn't care. He was spared from talking about it further when Willow's phone rang. "Hello?" she answered.

Hank pulled his own phone out of his pocket, texting "good morning" to Callie. But a few seconds later he heard a chime somewhere in the vicinity of the sofa. Rolling over to take a look, he found Callie's phone wedged between two of the cushions.

Across the room, the baby had her little fingers in Willow's hair, trying to get at her mother's phone. Willow turned her head as far as possible to resist her. "We'd be happy to be there at eleven," she said, craning away from Finley's questing fingers.

Hank rolled toward her and offered the baby his phone. Her big blue eyes went wide as she stretched with sturdy little arms toward him. Hank scooped her up and gave her the phone. He tucked Finley onto his lap, and Willow turned to mouth "thank you."

Finley clutched his phone in her fat little hands. Hank rolled over to the floor-to-ceiling window and looked outside. Sure enough, a few flurries had already appeared in the air. Even though the snow was really no use to him, his heart kicked at the sight. A year ago, those first flakes would have found him digging his equipment out of the storage shed he'd built to hold it all. Some thoughtful family member had removed all his goggles and helmets from the closets after the accident. But all it took was a few flakes of snow to put him in touch with the ghosts of winters past.

Hank turned around to find Willow watching him. "She suits you," Willow said, tucking her phone into her back pocket.

"Sorry?"

"The baby. You make a cute pair."

He chuckled. "That's because we both wear our hair short." He dropped a hand onto Finley's wispy little head. She was warm to the touch and smelled of baby powder.

"We're having another one," Willow volunteered.

"*Really*," Hank drawled. "You mean, eventually?"

"No, I mean in June."

"You kids are quite productive."

"We're doing our level best," Willow smiled. He laughed. "Callie must be over the moon. I know how much she likes this one." Ouch. There she was again, right in the front of his mind.

"She was pretty surprised," Willow said. "But she likes babies. A lot."

Hank had no reply to that. There was little chance he'd ever get the chance to hear Callie's opinions on parenthood if she kept running off.

"I think she's panicking a little bit," Willow continued.

You don't say.

"...She thinks she's running out of time."

Hank snorted. "Not hardly."

"I know that. But Callie likes to plan her life seventeen steps in advance. That's the only way to become a doctor. You can't just sail wherever life takes you. She's had to keep a firm hand on the rudder."

"She's afraid of me, then."

"Terrified," Willow agreed. "Good thing that yesterday her jerk-face ex basically offered to pick up where he left off with Callie."

Something lurched in Hank's gut. "What?"

Willow grinned at him. "Don't worry. She told him where he could shove that idea. That's how I know you've gotten under her skin."

At least that was something.

"While I was on the phone, Callie emailed to ask if she'd left her phone here."

Hank pulled it out of his pocket and showed it to Willow.

"Do you want me to drop it off at the hospital when I go into town?"

"Nah. I'll get it to her," he said.

"Smart man."

Hank put one hand on the baby's belly and one hand on his left wheel. Then he gave his chair a good yank, so that they turned around in a tight circle. The baby rewarded him with a giggle. So he did it again.

"Aw," Willow said. "She likes you."

"All the girls like me," Hank quipped. *All except for the one I need.*

Hank blew off his therapy session to take Dane and Willow out to breakfast. After they'd left town, he thought about stopping by the hospital to see Callie. But that wasn't really the best place to talk. So he waited until evening to try to find her.

She wasn't at home, so he ended up heading to the hospital after all. He parked his car, assembled his wheelchair and went inside. The therapy rooms were deserted. She wasn't in her office. Tiny wasn't around, either. Nobody at the nurse's station had seen her in hours. She wasn't working a night shift.

He was out of ideas.

As Hank drove back into town, the roads were getting noticeably messy. Still, he couldn't stand the thought of going home to more hours in his house alone. He drove to Rupert's bar instead. The closer he got to the place, the better the idea sounded. If his sister was working, he could drink as much as he wanted. And she would have to drive him home in the Jeep after her shift.

Giddyup.

Also, he found a handicapped parking spot on Main Street, so it was definitely meant to be. (Taking those spots guilt-free was absolutely the only good thing about his injury.)

This time when he assembled his wheelchair, it was in two inches of fluffy new snow. And the air smelled of more. Funny how he'd never really noticed before that snow had a scent. But it did. Cold and crisp, with just a hint of pine and wood smoke. That's what winter smelled like.

He rolled into the bar. Monday night football was on TV, and a smattering of patrons lined the bar. Hank's eye snagged on one particularly large head.

"Tiny!" Hank called.

"Hazardous!" the big man returned with a grin. But he was holding his phone to his ear, so Hank would have to wait a minute to catch up with him.

The open seat beside Tiny had a jacket on it. But to the left of that one there was a free bar stool. Hank didn't want to sit at a table alone, so with a press and a twist, he yanked his body onto the stool. So long as he didn't drink too much, he wouldn't roll off.

"That was pretty decent," a voice said from behind. "But the Russian judge held back a point from your score. Because she's ornery like that."

Hank looked over his shoulder at his sister. "Hey! You didn't come over last night. I thought you didn't have to work?"

Stella shrugged. "I needed a night at home, you know? What did I miss?"

Well, Sis, it was the best night of my life, right up until the point where it wasn't anymore. "You know—beer and cigars. Willow and Dane say hello, by the way. Bear brought over the itinerary for his film shoots. I read it over this afternoon. Looks like fun."

"I'll bet it does," she grumbled. "What do you want to drink?"

"Did you memorize the beer list yet?"

His sister gave him the stink eye.

"Surprise me, then."

Stella moved off in a huff, dragging his chair along with her.

"Your sister cracks me up," Tiny said, tucking his phone into his jacket pocket.

"Yeah?" Hank asked, offering Tiny a fist bump.

"Callie introduced me."

"Callie?"

"What?" Callie appeared suddenly at Hank's elbow.

Hank gave her a quick head-to-toe inspection, because something was not quite right. She looked a little fuzzy around the edges. When he lifted his eyes to Tiny's, the man gave Hank a wink.

Ah. Callie was half in the bag.

"Have a seat," Hank said, fighting a smile. He took her elbow gently and angled her toward the bar stool.

"Earlier, Callie informed me that tonight would be Tequila Night," Tiny said, taking her other elbow. "Although she won't say why."

Callie shrugged both their hands away. "I didn't hear any objections from you," she said. Then she waved Travis over.

"And how often does Callie declare Tequila Night?" Hank asked lightly.

"Not often," Travis put in, removing her empty glass. "She's more of a just-one-beer-for-me-thanks kind of customer."

"You're very patronizing. All of you," Callie muttered.

"Can I get you something, Hazardous?" Travis asked, amusement in his eyes.

"I asked my sister to pick out a beer for me. There's at least half a chance she'll remember."

"But it's Tequila Night," Callie said.

"A doctor once told me to stay away from tequila."

Callie's expression darkened. "Good point. Your doctor is the worst influence ever. Total disaster."

Okay. So that had not been the right thing to say. "I think that doctor is too hard on herself. And I'm not her patient anymore. Hey, Trav? Can I have a shot of Conmemorativo? But make it a single. I think I'm going to be driving somebody home in a little while."

"I can do that," Tiny said lightly. "My participation in Tequila Night has been nominal."

"I'm thinking I should do the honors."

"Sounds like a bad idea," Callie said, looking down at her hands.

With a curious expression, Tiny studied them both before wisely deciding to say nothing.

Travis put a shot down in front of Hank, and a margarita in front of Callie. To Tiny, he served a soda.

"How many of those has she had?" Hank asked. He tossed back his shot.

"I'm right here," Callie said, exasperated. "You could just ask *me*."

"That's her fourth," Travis said. "But the formula changes each time. I really just waved the tequila over that one."

"You're watering down my drinks?" Callie yelped. "What kind of a bartender are you?"

"The kind you'll be thanking when it's time to go to work in the morning."

"I hate you all. Well, maybe not Tiny."

"*Maybe?*" Tiny asked, clutching his heart.

"That's a shame," Hank said. "Because we think pretty highly of you."

"Don't sweet-talk me, Hank. That only leads to trouble."

He chuckled. "You were supposed to call me today, lady."

Callie took a sip of her drink before answering. "I can't find my phone."

"I see. And were there no other phones to be had?"

She took a gulp of the margarita and didn't meet his eyes.

He dug her phone out of his pocket and showed it to her. "Does this look familiar? It turned up between the cushions of my sofa."

While Tiny's eyes went wide, Callie made a wild grab for the phone. Hank held it out of her grasp. "Sorry, I'm holding this hostage."

"Jesus," Callie swore. "You're going to get me fired."

"No, I'm not," he said. "That sounds like a handy excuse to bail on me."

"It is not an excuse!" she said at a decibel level that everyone in the bar probably heard. "Do you know how much student-loan debt I have? Two hundred grand."

She made another lunge for the phone, but Hank caught her questing hand in his. "All right," he said in a calm voice. "That's more than a trifle. But are you actually sure that you and I are a punishable offense?"

"Nope," Callie said, stifling a burp. "But I'm worried enough to declare Tequila Night."

And to be fair, Callie did look as shaken up as Hank had ever seen her. "The last guy only got an ice cream binge, so maybe that means something good for me." He massaged her palm with his thumb. Her eyes went soft then, and so the tightness in his gut began to relax. Just a little.

"There will be plenty of time for ice cream, too," Callie whispered. "The hospital director is away at a conference."

"You tried to see her?"

"First thing this morning. Well, not *first* thing. Because I've been up since four worrying about what she'll say."

Okay. Hank could work with that. He woke up Callie's phone and began sifting through her contacts. Doctor Fennigan's number was right there in the Fs, because that was just the sort of organized girl Callie was.

He tapped her name and watched as the call attempted to connect.

"What are you doing?" Callie grabbed his wrist.

"It's ringing," he said. "Even if you hang up now, she'll still see that you tried to call."

"Hello?" A voice could be heard from the phone. Hank handed it to Callie.

Callie gave Hank a look so piercing that it could be used to sharpen snowboards. Then she stuck the phone to her ear. "Um...Dr. Fennigan? Sorry about the awkward timing." She gave Hank another evil look as she struggled off the bar stool and out the door.

"You are in so much trouble," Tiny said, draining his Coke.

"Probably true," Hank admitted.

"At least I know now why Tequila Night was necessary." Tiny shrugged on his jacket. "I'm going to let you take it from here."

"You don't have to go, man," Hank said. "Didn't mean to make you uncomfortable."

"You didn't," Tiny said, zipping up. "But if I hurry, I can still catch my friends. I blew them off because Callie spent the whole day looking like a grenade with the pin loose. I thought I was going to have to set her up in front of the heavy bag." He winked.

"You're a good man, Tiny. Next time, you don't even have to let me win the pull-up contest."

Tiny rolled his eyes. "I wish that was intentional. Later."

With her phone clutched to her ear, Callie hurried out of the bar and into the snowy night.

"Is something the matter?" The director asked.

"Hi, Doctor Fennigan," Callie said, cringing. She spoke slowly in the hopes that the director wouldn't guess that she'd been keeping company with several margaritas. "I'm sorry to call in the, uh, evening hours. But I needed to ask you to clarify something you said earlier."

The director chuckled. "Is this about Hank Lazarus?"

"It might be." God, she was such a wimp. "It *is*," she corrected. "You said he wasn't my patient, and I know that's strictly true. But that doesn't mean it would be proper for me to date him." And *date* was a heck of a euphemism at this point.

There was a silence on the other end of the line, and Callie hated the sound of it. "Let's think this through," the director said. "During the course of your week, do you provide medical treatment to any of the study participants?"

"Never. The head of the therapy department does that. My

role is only to observe and collect data. But I'd never want anyone to say that our study is flawed because of my personal relationships."

"Callie, did you happen to look up this issue in our employee handbook?"

"No." She swallowed hard.

"Well, it does *not* say that a doctor who senses a romantic relationship developing with her patient will be executed by firing squad."

Callie swallowed. "That's good to know."

"It advises the doctor to seek guidance from her superiors, and to terminate the professional relationship."

"Okay?"

"Right now you're seeking guidance, so that's covered. And now I'm going to temporarily relieve you of operating the study, until we can work through these questions together."

Callie gulped. "Okay."

"Even if we decide that another employee should take over for you, I can't think of any reason why you couldn't coauthor the results next year. At that point, the study participants will be numbers on a page."

"Thank you." *I think.* Callie exhaled, still rattled. Because it couldn't possibly be that easy. "Doctor Fennigan…"

"Elisa."

"Elisa, are you *sure* there's no way I could get in trouble for dating Hank? My job is very important to me."

The director was quiet for a moment before answering. "There's always a worst-case scenario. Suppose a relative of Hank's decides to hate you, or one of the study participants gets pissed at the hospital for some reason—there's always a chance that someone with an ax to grind will make a big stink over whatever they can find to work with. You could end up on the wrong side of a newspaper article. But the thing is, that could happen even if you *didn't* pursue a relationship with Hank, true?

"Right?" Callie's head hurt from trying to guess all the possibilities.

"There's always something to go wrong. But that's life. The one thing I'm certain of is that we spend our best years inside that hospital building. And if the right man wanders through those doors, we can't dismiss him out of hand. Because hotties driving red sports cars aren't just falling from the sky."

Callie let out a laugh that hopefully did not sound too soaked with tequila. "No, they're not. I just wish it weren't so complicated."

"You'll figure it out, I'm sure. Good night, Callie."

"Good night, Elisa."

Callie disconnected. For a moment, all she could do was stand there in the cold, letting the snow continue to coat her hair. It was falling in earnest now. Director Fennigan had not said what Callie had expected her to say. And while she felt relieved that the director was not horrified by her dalliance with Hank, the way forward was still not obvious.

She tipped her eyes upward, revealing a pattern of whirling white flakes illuminated by the streetlights. "Can't I get a little sign?" she asked the empty street. "Just a nod from God that it will all turn out okay?"

But as she watched the whirling snow, and tried to listen to her heart, all she received in answer was a very fat snowflake landing squarely in her eye. Blinking, Callie pulled open the door to the bar. Shaking snow out of her hair, she walked back into the warmth of Rupert's, and the sounds of laughter and football. Hank's pleasantly bulky form was there, muscular forearm on the bar, his head cocked to see the score on the screen. The sight of Hank waiting for her gave Callie's heart gave an involuntary shimmy.

Not so fast, atria and ventricles. No matter how irresistible she found Hank, she was still mad. Striding up to where he sat at the bar, she delivered a very sharp smack to his shoulder.

"Ow," he complained, his eyes still on the TV. "What's that for?"

"You *know* what that's for. You forced me to out myself to the hospital director." When he turned to face her, she smacked him again. "Not nice."

"Ouch," he repeated. "That hurts." But he proceeded to rub the *opposite* arm, as a cocky smile lit his face.

"You know, punching works better," Stella Lazarus said as she came by with an empty tray. On her way past, she made a fist and nailed her brother in the shoulder.

But Hank ignored her. Moving fast, he hooked his hands around Callie's jaw and pulled her forward, drawing her into an aggressive kiss.

Unready and off balance, Callie could mount no defense against those full lips. Hank gave a grunt of pleasure as he invaded her mouth, his tongue sweeping against hers with no preamble. Tipped into his chest, she found herself holding on instead of pushing back. The combination of alcohol and a lusty kiss made her hearing swimmy and indistinct. Even so, she picked up one or two cat calls in the background, and the sound of Stella Lazarus telling them to get a room.

Just when Callie's knees began to go squishy, the kiss ended almost as abruptly as it began. Gripping Hank's jacket for support, she felt drunker than at any other point in the evening.

"I'm going to take you home now," he said.

That helped to shake her out of her trance. "No, you're

not." She couldn't put last night on replay. When she'd decided to get drunk tonight, the plan wasn't meant to include him. Alcohol and Hank were potentially devastating, a combination so potent that the dosage was impossible to calibrate. "Where's Tiny? He's waiting to take me home."

Hank dropped some bills onto the bar. "He went out the back. Said to tell you good-night. Hey—Stella! Since you never brought me a beer, can you at least bring me my wheels?"

"Whoops. Sorry," his sister said as she scurried to the corner to get his wheelchair.

When it arrived, he dropped into it. "Come on. My car is out in front."

Callie watched the snowflakes swirl in front of Hank's headlights. "Can you even drive a Porsche in the snow?" The brain-scrambling kiss had left her feeling the need to be a little catty. As if arguing with Hank would help her keep her defenses engaged.

"Lady, my baby has four-wheel drive and snow tires." Hank sounded a bit miffed at the suggestion that his car wasn't manly enough for the task.

Callie sank back into the luxurious seat. The car smelled deliciously of leather upholstery and Hank. So...sexy.

Argh. When it came to him, her defenses were faulty. Always.

They rode along in silence, the lights of town fading away behind them. "I was already going to speak to Dr. Fennigan. You didn't have to force the issue."

"I know you were," he said, his voice a sexy rumble. "I just accelerated the conversation."

"Because a girl who only gets drunk twice a year really wants to talk to her boss on Tequila Night."

His laugh was dry. "You could probably perform neurosurgery drunk, Callie. And I wasn't going to let you wait a week to talk to her. That's too much time for you to climb back into that pretty head of yours, and think up a dozen more reasons why I'm a bad idea."

"I don't do neurosurgery," Callie pointed out. Hank chuffed out a laugh, and the car began a slow climb up a mountain road.

"Are you going to tell me what she said?" Hank asked, his eyes on the road.

"I haven't decided." She peered out the window, looking for familiar landmarks. But there weren't any. "This isn't the way to my house."

"And who said you were impaired by alcohol? It's the way to mine."

"Hank! What the hell? Stop the car."

As soon as she said it, he pulled into a strange driveway, stopping when they were just off the road. Silently, he turned to her, one eyebrow cocked questioningly.

Callie crossed her arms over her chest. "I'm still mad at you."

"What did Fennigan say?"

She called you a hottie. "She took me off the study."

He lost his cocky expression then. "Oh, shit. I'm sorry."

That admission of guilt ought to have made her feel better. But it only made it harder to stay mad. "That's all right," she said. "I deserved it. And I was expecting worse."

"You didn't do anything wrong," Hank said, his voice soft. "When I *was* your patient, you turned me down right away."

"But sometimes it doesn't matter whether you sinned or not. It only matters whether people think you did. You also outed me to Tiny tonight, and that was *before* I got to speak to Elisa."

"Yeah," Hank admitted. "But Tiny would never throw you under the bus. I think he'd lay down in the road, first. People love you, Callie. You get the benefit of the doubt, because you deserve it."

That was just about the nicest thing anyone had ever said to her. But it was also just plain optimistic. "I'm not brave," she said.

"I know." He reached across the gearbox to take her hand. "You told me that during *Silence of the Lambs*."

She squeezed his hand, wishing that life were easier, so that she'd never have to let go. "I'm not brave. But also, you're not ready."

"For what?"

"For me."

"What's that supposed to mean?"

"You've had such a tough year, and you're not ready to… to…*commit*." As soon as the word left her mouth, she was sorry she'd said it. It was too much to ask of him.

"Says who?"

"Look, don't deny this. If it weren't for your accident, I wouldn't be your choice, okay? I'm not your type. I've never been your type. And I don't want to be the one who cares too much, and have you be the one who settled."

She felt his hand go tight in hers. "Shit, that is *so* unfair. When *my* fear got in the way, you called bullshit. And now you're pulling the same crap on me? What's the point of playing that game—trying to guess whether we'd have ever met? We're great together. We've had a real connection since the first time you walked into my hospital room." He took a deep breath. "It's not fair for you to pretend you don't feel it, or that it doesn't matter."

The anger in his voice made her heart beat faster. "Hank,"

she said quietly. "I think you have no idea who you want. You just got your life back, and I hear that you're grateful to me. And God knows I'm so happy for you. But you could have anyone."

"And so could you! What does that have to do with anything? Maybe we would have found each other, anyway. Don't pretend like you know."

She swallowed, feeling dizzy. She did know, actually.

"What?"

She shook her head.

"Callie, level with me—it's really the least you can do." He took his hand back, gripping the steering wheel instead.

"You're going to say I'm reading too much into it."

"Try me."

"Hank, we *did* meet. On the worst day of your life, Dane and Willow introduced me to you."

His dark eyebrows shot up. "Oh, fuck. Really?" Closing his eyes, he pinched the bridge of his nose. He was silent for a minute. "Damn. It was right before my run."

Callie stopped breathing.

His chin snapped up to look at her. "I asked Dane where we were drinking later. And I made a crack about his being whipped." He chuckled, but then there was pain in his eyes. "You had on a bright pink hat." He reached across to place one hand on the crown of her head. "It covered your hair, and I wondered what color it was. And Dane was holding the baby." The fingers that he brought up to touch his lips were shaking. "And I was such an asshole."

"It was a stressful moment..."

"That's not why I said the things I said." He gave his head a shake. "I was so jealous, Callie. It was my hometown mountain—it was supposed to be such a big day for me. And a big year. But my bitchy girlfriend had just given me the 'look, when you get back, we need to talk,' speech. And my buddy Dane is standing there, and he has everything. There was a family standing beside him. He figured it all out, and I was just floundering." He took a long, shaky breath. "So if you think you know how it was with me then... Well, lady. You don't know a thing."

Callie was so surprised that she had to remind herself to breathe. "*Hank,*" she whispered, leaning across the gearbox, gathering him in as best she could. "I'm so sorry. I didn't get it. It's just that you looked like someone who had everything he wanted."

"I'm telling you to your face, Callie, things I never told anyone before. I can't make it any clearer than I'm making it now."

"Okay, okay," she soothed. "That was stupid of me. I was afraid to have my heart broken."

He wrapped her in powerful arms. "You know, I might not have been ready to meet you a year ago." He kissed the top of her head. "But I was getting there. The accident wasn't the only reason. I was coming to the end of wanting to be young and stupid."

She squeezed him again. "You say that like it's a bad thing. Sometimes I worry that I was never young and stupid enough. It's like I've been trying to make up for it now, acting like a crazy lady."

"I can help you with that. I do stupid and crazy really well." He rocked her gently. "I want you, Callie. And you want me. Nothing else matters."

"California," she said.

His arms held her even tighter. "Stop."

"You said if I mentioned it again, you would..."

She didn't get the words out, because his lips covered hers. The kiss was slow, smoldering with the promise of even hotter things to come.

When they finally came up for air, Hank was perfectly silent for a long minute. In the dashboard lighting, his serious face took on a wizened expression. "Vermont is going to wake up to a powder day tomorrow. But I was hoping to wake up next to you."

"I'd like that."

Hank put the car in gear. Callie sat back in her seat, and he pulled onto the road again. It was only a couple more minutes until they rolled into his garage. Hank opened the driver's side door. He had to put his chair together one more time. That took a couple of minutes, so he handed her his key. "Here. You choose which side of the bed you want to sleep on. Choose carefully, because it's not just for tonight." He reached into the backseat for a wheel.

With a full heart, Callie did.

CHAPTER
EIGHTEEN

CALLIE WOKE up the next morning to the press of a hard wall of muscle at her back. She lay still for a moment, taking stock. Hank's hand was draped over her hip, his fingers splayed out on the sensitive skin of her belly. She was dressed in one of Hank's big T-shirts. This one had a double-black-diamond symbol on the front, beneath the words *Experts Only*.

That was, however, the only thing she was wearing. Last night, they'd made slow, sleepy love curled together much as they were right this minute. Just thinking about it gave Callie a warm tingle.

And Hazardous was a cuddler. Who knew?

Callie lifted her head an inch to peer at Hank's clock. It was eight-thirty already. She should be headed to the hospital by now. At the very thought, a spear of anxiety sliced through her head. Because no matter how many lovely things had happened last night, her career had been altered by a single, drunken phone call to the hospital director. At the thought, her head began to thrum with worry.

Or maybe that was the hangover talking.

The warm hand that had been draped onto her belly began to move. It squeezed her hip. Then it traveled gently around back, tracing circles at her waist. Closing her eyes, Callie lay still. No matter how complicated the day would get, she would take this moment to appreciate the feel of Hank's fingertips on her skin. It would be easy to get used to this kind of affection. "Callie," he whispered.

She rolled over, and her first sight was a panorama of his impressive chest. She let her gaze drift slowly upward, past the six-pack to the inked shoulders. When she reached his face, she expected to find an amorous look in his eye. But what she saw was something else.

Intensity.

"What's the matter?" she asked, reaching out to brush a hand past the morning whiskers on his jaw.

Hank propped his head on his hand, regarding her seriously. "I just realized. You saw it happen."

"What?"

"If I met you at the ski mountain that means you saw me break. Callie, you *watched*." His eyes were dark pools, boring into hers.

She reached out again, touching his chest, measuring the hard press of muscle under her hand. He was so difficult to read right now. He seemed almost angry. "I was there," was all she could think to say. It was the truth, whether he liked it or not. "It's not my fondest memory."

"But you're here now."

She blinked at him, caressing the sunburst tattoo under her hand. "Of course I am."

He reached out with both hands, hauling Callie into his embrace. "You really are amazing."

"Why?" She nuzzled the skin just beneath his ear.

"Because you want me anyway," he said, arranging her on his chest. "I just..." He let out a big breath. "A lot of my old friends look at me, and I can just see the wheels turning. They're making the comparison. Doesn't matter what we're talking about—the Patriots, the weather. They're thinking, *that poor slob. Look at him now.* You never look at me that way, and I thought it was because you didn't have a reference point. I thought you never saw the real me."

Callie popped up so that she could look down into his eyes. "No, I've *got* the real Hazardous." She cupped his chin with one hand. "He's right here."

Hank didn't say anything. But his eyes shone with such depth and wonder that it made her heart swell to see it. Callie dropped her head onto his shoulder, and his arms encircled her again. He returned to stroking her back, while Callie listened to the thud of his heart through his chest.

"We should probably get up," she said after a time. "I have to go to the hospital and figure out if I still have a job."

"Of course you still have a job. But they haven't put you back on the regular schedule yet, right?"

Callie knew he had a point. It's just that Dr. Callie didn't lounge in bed when her future was uncertain. It was almost a physical need—to park in the doctor's lot, and make sure that her ID card still opened all the important doors. In the bright light of morning, giving up the study was terrifying. She'd put it on the resume she'd sent to California. How would she explain that she was no longer part of the project? The familiar hum of anxiety she always carried with her began to buzz in her ears.

"It's a snow day, baby." Hank rubbed her back again, and the heat of his hands began to smooth down the harshest edges of her worry. "We're going to drink some coffee, and

then we're going to do my second favorite thing in the world."
As he said it, he reached under her T-shirt again and cupped
her breast. When his thumb slid over her nipple, the worry
train in her mind hopped the tracks.

Holy hell. Callie melted into him.

"Aren't you going to ask me what that is?" Hank chuckled.
"My second favorite thing?"

"Hmm...?" Callie asked, not really caring about the
answer. As long as it involved Hank, and the rich sound of his
laugh, and the warmth of his hands.

"We're going to the ski mountain, of course." The warm
hands fell away. Rolling onto his back, Hank grabbed the land-
line off his night table.

Callie caught his hand before he could dial. "Seriously?"
She would have thought it was the last place he'd want to go.
Hank shook her off and tapped one of the speed dial buttons.
"Yo, Stella," he said a minute later. "Are you going over to the
hill?"

Because she was lying practically on top of Hank, she could
hear a thin version of his sister's answer. "Do you even have to
ask? I got the call at six this morning. It's all hands on deck."

Hank paused. "Except mine, I guess."

Stella didn't answer right away. "Did you really expect to
get that call? Who would ask that of you? But hey—you're free
to take my place," Stella offered. "I'll take the powder day, and
you can sell season passes."

When Hank chuckled Callie heard it through his chest.
"Kind of you to offer, but let's do it the other way around. Do
you know where all my winter gear went? Callie and I are
going to need goggles, helmets and snow pants."

"I guess I can dig through the parents' closets on the way
over. You're not going to try out your new toy already?"

"You bet."

"Don't tell Mom," Stella said. "She'll worry."

"What are we, twelve?"

"You don't want to be grounded like me."

"Eh. I'm good at sneaking out."

Through the phone, Callie heard Stella's laughter. "That you are."

"See you over there, Sis." He disconnected the call.

"What are you plotting?" Callie asked.

He reached under the covers and gave her ass a playful smack. "You'll see. But first, we need coffee."

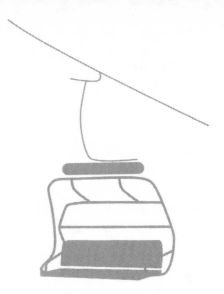

CHAPTER
NINETEEN

HANK LISTENED to Callie curse under her breath as the chairlift swung around into position behind them. "Ready?" he asked, biting back a laugh.

"No!"

"She's fine," Bear promised.

When the bench approached, Hank pressed down hard on the two specially designed ski poles in his hands, lifting the seat of his sit-ski (and therefore his ass) a few crucial inches into the air. He felt the lift catch him underneath, and then they were flying—slowly—over the bunny hill. Hank reached back to tug on the back of the chairlift, making sure he and his new contraption weren't going to slip off.

"There aren't even seat belts," Callie muttered from the other side of Bear. "How is this legal?"

Hank tipped his head back, allowing more of the morning sunlight to warm his face. "The bigger question is how a girl could have grown up a couple of hours from Lake Tahoe without ever learning how to ski or ride?"

"Seriously," Bear echoed. "That's just plain wrong."

When they'd arrived at the hill an hour ago, Callie had flat-out refused to try a snowboard. "I don't want to feel like my feet are tied together," she'd insisted. "Actually, I don't want to slide downhill at all. But if I'm going to do it, I'm doing it on skis."

Then Bear—who was either the best friend on the entire planet or bending over backward to get Hank to do his movie —had actually rented a pair, too.

"I thought you were a snowboarder," Callie had said as they struggled into the stiff boots.

"Yeah," Bear had said with a wink. "I guess you could say I swing both ways."

And now all three of them were gliding up the hill, an impossibly blue sky overhead. It was a Tuesday in November, which meant that the only people on the hill were local kids who'd been granted the gift of an early snow day. And all of them had been skiing since preschool. The bunny hill would be deserted.

Conditions were perfect for terrifying Callie.

"How shall we play this?" Bear asked as the end of the bunny lift appeared.

"Maybe I could just ride back down," Callie suggested.

Hank grinned. "Not a chance. Bear, just give me a shove, and then see if you can keep Callie vertical."

"Might work," Bear agreed.

Then the landing was upon them. Hank leaned forward and felt himself disengage from the chair. He put his odd ski poles down to meet the ground—they had little skis on their bottoms—and glided forward, the monoski underneath him skimming over the snow.

Callie shrieked, so he swiveled his torso to look for her. And that did him in. The sit-ski tipped, and he went down.

But Hank had only to dig the back of one ski pole into the snow and lever himself upright again.

That wasn't so bad.

Balancing now, he poled away from the lift area and waited while Bear helped Callie to her feet.

She shuffled awkwardly forward, a grim expression on her face.

"Now, remember," Bear coached. "Parallel skis make you go fast. Wedge your toes together when you want to slow down. When they teach this to kids, they say that 'french fries' are for 'go' and 'pizza' is for 'stop.'"

"Pizza it is, then," Callie grumbled. "Where do I go?"

Hank pointed in the obvious direction. "Down."

He watched while Callie, her legs quirked into the awkward stance of the terrified, pushed her skis into a wedge and eased down the bunny hill. Hank put two fingers into his mouth and whistled. "That's it, baby!"

She fell down about a second later.

Bear swooped in to help her up, and they began again.

For a few minutes, Hank sat alone at the top of the little rise, just watching them. But eventually Bear stopped to lift his chin, checking on him. "Are you sure you want to do this?" Bear had inquired when Hank asked for the sit-ski to be brought out of storage.

"Sure," Hank had said, voicing more conviction than he felt. "Piece of cake."

It was probably the biggest lie he'd voiced in his life.

Now Hank looked down at his equipment, wondering what the hell he'd been thinking.

Last spring, his snowboarding sponsors had all cut him off, one by one. Their checks had stopped arriving. And for the first time in years, Hank was no longer supporting himself.

But his favorite sponsor—a helmet manufacturer—had sent along the sit-ski, with a note. *We don't know whether you'll want this, or when you'll be ready for it. But we'd like you to have it just in case. P.S. Always wear your helmet.*

Was he ready? Who knew. But, ready or not, he was seated above a metal crutch of sorts, which put his ass a couple of feet off the snow. His legs were zipped together in front of him on a footrest. Underneath this getup was a single ski. For balance and mobility, he had two multi-purpose poles. Now he rocked a little from side to side, trying to get a feel for the balance of the thing. To steer, he was meant to tip his hips either left or right, edging the ski into the snow. The whole thing looked unwieldy. But people actually raced on these things in the Paralympics. How hard could it be?

He looked down the hill, and his heart rate kicked up a notch. This was his first time on the snow since *that* day. And it had all happened a few hundred yards from here. That's why Hank had come out here today, on the very first ski day of the season. If he didn't try this today, the moment would only grow in importance. Every day he didn't do it would just make the problem bigger.

And right now, every minute he sat up here thinking about it did the same.

Fuck.

Without any more preparation, Hank shoved forward on his poles and leaned downhill. The ski beneath him did its job, its waxed surface compressing the snow underneath, propelling him forward. And then gravity had its say, too. Hank began to accelerate. He leaned a bit to the right, experimenting with steering. Not a whole lot happened, except that Hank began to travel downhill even faster. So Hank leaned farther, edging the ski into the snow. He turned, hard, and quickly skidded to a fall, a plume of snow rising up around him. He landed on his forearm, the ski poles clattering around into his sit-ski contraption. And then it was quiet.

Well, okay then. He had falling all figured out.

Hank fished the ski pole out from under his body and levered himself up and vertical again. Even though his heart was hammering, he didn't wait. Pointing the ski downhill, he immediately made a gentle turn to the left. That seemed to go okay, so he made another one to the right. Left again. Right. He steered around a guy who was putting up a sign that read Slow: Learning Area.

He picked up some speed, but it wasn't welcome just yet. So he made his next turn a deeper one and slowed himself down. *That's it. Nice and easy. Left... Right...* He'd forgotten how this felt—to lose himself completely in a physical activity. His mind was cleared of everything that wasn't the snow, the ski and two poles. No thinking allowed.

Before he was ready for it to end, Hank surprised himself by arriving at the bottom of the hill. Using the momentum that gravity had provided, he made a careful arc around the chair-lift loading area. Then he stopped, planting both poles down for balance, and rested. He was breathing harder than he would have guessed.

Two thirds of the way up the little hill, Bear and Callie stood together. Bear was gesturing with his hands, probably teaching Callie some valuable nugget of ski wisdom.

They looked like they'd be a while, so Hank poled forward into the loading area. The lifty hit the lever and slowed the chairs down to half speed. Now *that* was mortifying. Nobody had slowed a chairlift down for him since he'd graduated from kindergarten. On the other hand, falling off the lift was not on his to-do list for today. So Hank decided not to worry about it.

When the chair came, he pulled himself on carefully and sat back for the ride.

Overhead, the sky was so blue that it almost hurt his eyes. And when Hank looked down, he could pick out the S-shaped turns he'd carved into the snow. And damn if that didn't put a big old lump in his throat.

He'd been two years old the first time he slid down this hill on little-kid skis. There was a picture somewhere of Hank skiing with a pacifier in his mouth. At seven, he'd traded up to a snowboard. He'd grown up right on this spot, eating chili and burgers in the ski lodge, watching bigger kids practice their tricks in the half-pipe.

His whole life had happened on these hills. As an adult he'd ridden his snowboard at every major resort in North America. But it had all started right here. And that's why it had been right and necessary to come here today. He couldn't be afraid of this place. He *wouldn't* be afraid.

At the top, he pushed himself off the lift this time, fumbling his hands onto the poles just quickly enough to avoid another crash on the dismount. On the crest, he paused to watch Callie skiing. She was doing a little better now, her body less tense. He saw her turn twice before falling in a puff of snow, legs akimbo. She flopped onto her back in the snow, dramatic but uninjured.

Smiling to himself, Hank pointed his ski in her general direction. It was a smoother trip this time, now that he had a better feel for the arc of the seat over the ski's edges. Taking care to keep his speed under control, he made it down to Callie in six or seven turns. He did a quarter turn around where she lay, used the uphill to kill his speed, and then pivoted to fall down into the snow beside her. "Come here often?" he asked her.

"What, like it's obvious?" she asked from flat on the ground.

Bear laughed. "You're getting better, I swear."

Hank pointed uphill. "You can take a run, dude. I want to talk to my girl."

With a shrug, Bear skied away.

"He's a very patient teacher," Callie said. "But his student is not very bright."

"I think she's pretty great."

Callie pulled herself up onto an elbow, her blue eyes taking him in. "Are you doing okay?"

Hank walked his forearms closer to her, and she took the hint, leaning in for the kiss. He laid one on her, and there was nothing subtle about that kiss. "I am doing great," he said against her lips. "And thank you for asking." He kissed her again, drawn in by her sweet taste.

"I saw you," she breathed between kisses. "It's not really fair that you can ski on that thing the first time out."

He ignored her complaint, kissing her more aggressively now. And the appreciative noise she uttered made Hank want to take his time.

"Mister, are you okay?"

Reluctantly, Hank pulled back from Callie and looked up. A little girl, maybe six years old, had paused on the ski slope, staring at them.

"Should I get the ski patrol?" the little creature asked.

"Nope. Nothing to see here," Hank said. "Move it along."

"Why don't you get up, then?" the little girl pressed, tilting her head to the side like a puppy. "Were you giving her CPR?"

"No!" Callie said, her tone full of horror. "Everything is fine. Really. Just, um, taking a little break."

"Bye, now," Hank tried, waving at her.

The little girl gave them one last suspicious glance and then skied off.

Callie met his eyes, and then they both laughed. But Callie's laugh turned into a groan, and she propped herself up on her elbows. "That last fall is going to leave a bruise. But at least I know who to turn to for CPR."

"I'm always available for mouth-to-mouth."

"Hank, there's a reason I never learned to ski," Callie said, rubbing a fist down her outer thigh. "And it wasn't fear."

"No?" He hoped she wouldn't be too sore from her ski lesson. Though if she was, he could always suggest that they fulfill one of his Jacuzzi fantasies.

She faced him again. "Squaw Valley was only a day trip from Sacramento. And in high school, my friends invited me to go with them. But the lift tickets and the equipment rental was over a hundred bucks. So I told them no."

"I see," Hank said. But now he felt like an ass. Every November, his parents had handed him a brand-new parka with a season pass tucked into the high-tech ID window on the upper arm. Their equipment shed was crammed full of late-model gear, which was traded in each time he and Stella grew out of the old stuff.

"Staying out of trouble at the hospital isn't just academic for me." Callie looked down at her hands. "I need that job. I've done well for myself, but it will still be a few years until I'm out of debt."

Hank cleared his throat. "I hope I didn't screw that up for you last night."

"I really don't think you did," she said immediately. "I'm just telling you why the idea of breaking the rules gives me the cold sweats. I don't *want* to be that boring girl. But I just can't afford to be reckless."

"The last thing you are is *boring*," Hank chuckled. Callie's chin snapped upward, and he could read on her face that she didn't believe him. "You're smart, and it's really sexy. I was always too much of an adrenaline junkie to stop and appreciate that in people. But there's more to life than jumping off stuff. You're the only woman I've met who makes me laugh every single day."

She actually blushed then, and looked away. "What is that guy doing?" she asked, pointing downhill.

In the center of the bunny slope, an employee stood with a shovel, scooping snow into a pile over a wedge-shaped wooden box.

"He's making a jump," Hank explained. "They make little terrain features here, to keep the kids out of the bigger terrain park. When I was a kid, I spent hours in my front yard, doing that. I had to build my own jumps. Now we do it for 'em."

"You won't make me jump today, will you?"

Hank shook his head. "Callie, I won't make you do anything. I'm just glad you came out here today with me. And tried it once." He reached down and unclipped himself from the sit-ski, shoving it away so he could sit more comfortably beside Callie.

She turned that blue gaze on him again. "I'll try skiing again. Really. I don't think I'll ever be *good* at it. But it's fun to do something badly once in a while. It takes you out of your own head, doesn't it?"

"Yeah," Hank whispered. Out of nowhere, he found himself almost choked up with appreciation for her. The journey he was on was not an easy one, yet she was on it, too. He hoped so anyway.

"Sometimes..." Callie said, her face grave. "...Sometimes I

dig my own ruts. I carve them nice and deep, and then I get stuck inside them."

Reaching for her hand, Hank yanked off one of the gloves that Stella had lent her. "I'll haul you out," he said. Then brought her palm up to his lips, kissing her.

When he looked up again, her eyes were brimming. "Would you?" Callie whispered. "I'd like that."

"Anytime, baby," Hank said, hitching closer so he could hug her. "Anytime."

They sat there on the hillside, holding one another as the lift turned in the distance, chair after chair crossing the blue sky. "You know," Hank said, his chin on Callie's shoulder. "I think I'm going to do Bear's film. There's nothing on his itinerary in California. But if you end up there, maybe I could convince him to shoot the last part at Tahoe."

"That won't be necessary," Callie replied. "If it's okay with you, I think I'll stay in Vermont for a while."

"I'm glad," Hank said. "Callie, don't kill me. But I realized this morning that I'm going to have to drop out of the study."

"What?"

"I'll call Dr. Fennigan to explain."

"Don't drop out, Hank. That's not the answer."

He shook his head. "I'm still going to do the therapy. But I can't be a study participant if I'm traveling for eight weeks this winter. Bear's itinerary is pretty fierce."

"Oh, crap. Your parents…"

"They'll be okay with it. The study will go on without me. I'll still ride the Frankenbike, and let Tiny do his worst to me whenever I'm in town. And maybe this makes it easier for you to keep your promotion."

"Hank, even if they take that away, I'll be okay with it. You're worth it."

His throat tightened up then. So he pulled Callie into his lap and held on tight. The several layers of clothing between their bodies were immaterial. He could still feel the warmth and the weight of her in his arms, and her breath on his neck. They were alive and well, and sitting on a ski slope in the sunshine.

A year ago he'd thought that everything had been taken from him on this hill. But that wasn't true anymore. Because something even greater had been given back. He felt heat behind his eyes, which only proved that he was turning into the world's biggest sap.

"I still have to ski down to the bottom, don't I?" Callie asked abruptly.

Hank tipped his head back to look into her eyes. "Are you scared?"

"A little. Turning is the hard part."

"I thought landing the jumps was the hard part."

She slapped his shoulder. "Show off."

"Easy, slugger." He caught her hand and kissed the palm. "Can I give you a tip?"

"Sure."

"The edges of your skis can't dig in if you're going really slow. It sounds counterintuitive, but you have to take a risk at faster speeds to make it work."

Callie turned to look downhill, thinking about it. "Isn't that always the truth."

"Pretty much."

She picked herself up off his lap and grabbed her ski poles. "Okay. Let's do this thing."

"I can't wait," Hank replied.

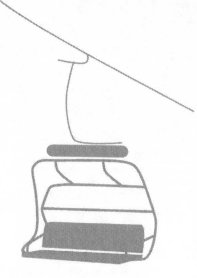

CHAPTER
TWENTY

ONE YEAR LATER

CALLIE WALKED into the little screening room in Park City, Utah, and did a quick scan. There were seats for about three-dozen people. Callie didn't know what she had been expecting, but it wasn't this—leather loungers that reclined in front of the big screen, and gourmet treat bags at every seat. It was fancy. Yet Bear and Hank's Park City friends, and the snowboard crew, still wore their trademark scruffy tees and beanies.

There was never a dull moment where Hank was concerned. You never knew exactly who or what would turn up. And Callie loved it all.

A few heads turned in her direction, and several hands waved hello. "Caddie!" a little voice yelled, and she turned to see Willow's toddler bouncing in her mother's lap. Beside them, Dane held their five-month-old son, Max. Since they were seated just behind Hank, Callie circled the room, dropping down onto the big double lounger beside her boyfriend.

She gave Hank's hand a squeeze, then spun around to blow a kiss to Finley, whom she had just seen at brunch an hour ago.

"Hey, Dane?" Callie asked. "If he wakes up, and you need someone to hold him during the film, I'll walk around with him." For now, the baby's chubby hands were curled into fists as he slept, and it took plenty of willpower not to reach over to stroke his soft skin.

"No, you won't," Hank insisted beside her, patting the leather seat. "I need you to watch this thing to the very end."

Callie sat down properly and turned to him. "I want to see your film," Callie said. "I just assume I'll be seeing quite a lot of it this year." The movie was going on tour to film festivals in some fun locations, and Callie was looking forward to using her vacation time to travel to France and Lake Tahoe with Hank.

Her godson, on the other hand, was a limited engagement in Callie's life.

Hank grabbed her hand again and kissed her knuckles. "Humor me," he said. "Watch the whole thing."

"All right," she said, catching a glimpse of his dark brown eyes. He really hadn't said a whole lot to her at brunch today. And, weirdly, he'd been reserved yesterday, too. Picking her up from the airport, he'd enveloped her in a tight hug. But afterward, the evening had been noticeably lacking in Hank-like conversation and bravado.

Callie felt a little chill, wondering why. "You've been awfully quiet this weekend. Is everything all right?" It wasn't like Hank to be nervous about the screening. That just wasn't his style.

"I'm good," he said, turning his attention to the screen, which had just flickered to life.

The house lights began to dim; Bear took a position at the

front of the room. "Friends," he began. "Neighbors. Sick, irresponsible snowboarders…"

There was a hoot from the audience and Callie grinned. They were a fun bunch, and she'd enjoyed getting to know some of them during the past year.

"…welcome, and thank you for coming out today to see the director's cut of the film. Hank and I had a blast making this movie with you. This version you're going to see today is the finished film, with the soundtrack completed, plus a few extra shots here and there. You'll know 'em when you see 'em." Bear winked, and then he sat down.

The screen lit slowly, showing a time lapse of the sun coming up over a mountain, as strains of music began to rise into the stillness. Callie watched, wide-eyed, as the first snowboarders swept onto the scene, flying off a clifflike jump and past the camera lens. To the pumping rhythm of a Red Hot Chili Peppers song, the trickery built, until the riders were throwing world-class aerials past the camera.

It was beautiful, but it left Callie with an uncomfortable sting in her heart. Her single visit to a half-pipe competition still haunted her. She wondered if that ache would ever go away—not just for her, but for Hank. He'd been so brave during the past year, getting outside with his pals, spending some time on the sit-ski, and even more time holding a camera. He never complained. But there had to have been times when it was torture.

Next, the film went on to document a big mountain foray. On screen, the snowboarders discussed whether it would be possible to ride down two previously uncharted Alaskan slopes.

Watching the film was a little like reliving the previous year. At the beginning, the work of filmmaking had been all discussion and planning. At Hank's dining table, he and Bear had hashed out their ideas. In the evenings after her hospital shifts, most nights she'd let herself in Hank's front door with the key he'd made her. When she walked into the room, his eyes would lift to find hers, illuminating with a hungry warmth that lit her up no matter how long the day had been.

Other nights, they went out together. Even though Callie had lived in Vermont for three years, Hank knew a lifetime's worth of secret spots. He took her snowmobiling under the full moon on the first clear, snowy night. Another time they drove an hour to an excellent pizzeria he knew in Chester. On one of her days off, they toured the Ben & Jerry's factory, where Callie looked down upon the machines that stirred cherries and chocolate into her favorite flavor. "I've arrived at the mother ship," she'd joked.

"Not that you're going to have another ice-cream crisis," Hank teased her. "But now you know where the magic happens." They took a selfie in front of a statue of a Holstein, and tasted a brand-new flavor.

Dating Hank was more fun than Callie had had in years.

On the big screen, the snowboarders had made it to Alaska, and into a helicopter. Even though she'd seen some of this footage before, Callie held her breath when the chopper lifted away, leaving three figures stranded on a rocky peak. And she gasped when the first one hopped his board right over the edge, seeming to stay vertical on the snowy cliff by force of will. The shots were both breathtaking in their beauty and danger. When the camera pulled back, each snowboarder looked to be ant-sized against the vast, stony mountain and the stormy gray skies.

The hardest bit to watch was the scene in which an avalanche began chasing one of the riders down the hill. Her grip tightened on Hank's wrist until he finally shook her off. "Callie," he whispered. "You just spoke to her."

"Oh, my God. That's *Stella?*" Callie tightened her grip again, even as Hank chuckled. Even though Callie knew the outcome, it was hard to watch the avalanche overtake Hank's sister, even if she did pop out of the snow a few seconds later, still on her board.

What sort of crazy people did this stuff, anyway?

Oh, right. All the people in this room.

When Hank had begun traveling for the film, Callie had put in extra hours at work in his absence. But she managed to get away to Idaho in February when the crew was shooting there. During the day in Sun Valley, when Hank was busy, Callie took private ski lessons from a very understanding instructor. But in the evenings, Hank left the movie crew and their dodgy accommodations to stay with her in a resort hotel room that he'd booked for the two of them. Together they'd indulged in fireside dinners, fine bottles of wine and enthusiastic hotel room sex.

If someone had told Callie the previous winter that in one year's time she'd be headed for a posh ski vacation with her sexy, athlete-turned-filmmaker boyfriend, she'd have never believed it. It had been a great winter, and an excellent year. She hoped Hank thought so, too.

But then why was he so quiet?

Callie sneaked a look at him in the darkness. His eyes were on the screen, but he was chewing his lip in a way that was not very Hank-like. The film continued on, covering other exotic locales and sparkling athlete personalities. But Callie's mind drifted, wondering what Hank was thinking.

The summer they'd just shared together had been amazing, too. With the filming done, Hank was around more often.

Hank and Bear spent long hours in the editing room, while Callie worked. But there was plenty of time for fun. They'd picked blueberries, and made another pie together. Hank took her to his parents' house, where she had been treated like a queen by Mr. and Mrs. Lazarus.

Hank took her fishing once, too. And although baiting hooks wasn't Callie's cup of tea, she enjoyed watching Hank reel one in. Hanging out with Hank was like *living* in an adventure movie, and she never wanted it to end. And it wasn't going to, was it?

Enough with being paranoid, Callie chided herself. The film was almost over, and she'd lost track of it, because she'd been too busy worrying to watch. Callie reached across the leather seat and took Hank's hand.

His fingers curled around hers reassuringly. "You're going to love this next part."

He was not wrong. The screen dissolved into a purely white world. Into the silence rose the noise of an engine. And then a snowmobile drove into the frame, bearing a single rider. And on his back, a violin case.

At Callie's gasp of surprise, Hank chuckled beside her.

On-screen Hank took out Willow's violin, tucked it under his chin and began to play an Irish reel. The sound was pure and lively. And after a few bars of music, a hip-hop rhythm kicked in underneath it. That was a neat trick—she'd have to remember to ask him how they'd done it. But then the camera began to pan backward. And the view revealed snowboarders *flying right over Hank's head!*

The snowmobile was parked between two snow features: one a take-off ramp, and the other for landing. As Hank played on, a series of boarders launched overhead, whirling around, landing inventive feats on the opposite side.

"Oh, my God," Callie breathed. "That looks so dangerous."

Hank snorted beside her. "Nah."

The camera panned out again, revealing a heavy sky. Eventually, the parade of tricksters ceased. One by one they rode out of sight, leaving Hank all alone in the shot. He and his invisible accompanists played a rollicking finale to the song, with the rhythm section ending first. And then Hank finished the tune, allowing the final note to ring out into the wind. On screen, it had just begun to snow.

Hank took the violin from his chin and stared up into the flakes. He packed the instrument in the case, and then slung it on his back. Then he cranked the snowmobile to life. With a tilt of his head, he circled the machine around in a wide arc. And before Callie could quite anticipate it, he gunned the engine. The snowmobile raced up the trick ramp. Callie stopped breathing as Hank launched the machine into the air. The film slowed down, drawing out the arc of his flight. The camera angle shifted to take in the sailing machinery from below.

The landing was accompanied by a sickening bounce. But Hank drove on, oblivious, racing off into the distance. Here the camera sped up, showing the lengthy zigzag of his departure in double time.

Callie was too startled to chime in as the people in the theater around her began to whistle and clap. She almost missed the fact that the film's credits began to roll, because her heart was still in her mouth.

Hank turned to her with a grin. "What did you think?"

She hesitated. *Careful*, an inner voice advised her. But… careful is precisely what Hank was not. "Did you *have* to jump that thing?" she blurted.

He threw his head back and laughed. Then he nudged her arm. "Keep watching."

Callie looked up at the screen again. The credits had ceased, and she saw an empty room. Hank rolled into view, stopping to turn his chair to face the camera. He held up one hand to an ear. "What's that, Callie? Did you just ask me why I had to jump the snowmobile?"

"Oh, for God's sake," Callie said aloud. And then everyone around her laughed.

On-screen Hank wasn't done. "Well, I'll tell you why. Because I *love* risk. Almost as much as I love you."

Callie's jaw fell open with surprise. And all around her, the audience said an exaggerated "Awwww!"

"…Which is why I can do this," on-screen Hank said. And then he reached his right hand into the air and began to write with one finger. "M A…" A bright blue line began to follow his finger, drawing in the letters where he'd put them in the air. "…R R Y M E…"

Callie's heart tripped over itself. Was he really…?

"C A L L I E" finished on-screen Hank.

"Oh, my GOD!" Willow yelled from the seat behind her.

On-screen Hank finished his writing, and crossed his arms over his chest. Callie turned, wide-eyed, to look at Real Hank, who wore a crooked little grin. And in his palm sat a little velvet box in robin's-egg blue. And in that box rested a gorgeous diamond solitaire.

For several beats of her heart, Callie could only stare at it. "Oh, Hank," she said finally. Gingerly, as if it might turn out not to be real, Callie took the box from his hand. "Is that for *me?*"

He grabbed her, pulling her into his lap. "Who else would it be for, you dope?" He kissed her hair. "Marry me, Callie."

Still silent, she blinked back happy tears. *Wow.* Words were clearly failing her. So she cupped Hank's masculine jaw in her hand and kissed him. Hard.

She felt his chuckle against her lips. "Are you going to answer the question, lady?"

"Yes."

"Yes, you're going to answer the question? Or…"

"Yes, Hank. Just… *yes*." She kissed him again. There was a roar of approval from the other two-dozen people in the room.

He met her lips eagerly, stoking the flame of her kisses into a blaze. But then he cupped her face in both his hands and softened the kiss. The tenderness she found there was just as breathtaking. He stilled his lips against her own, nuzzling her face with his. "I took you by surprise?"

She nodded against him. "Totally."

"Good. Do you like the ring? If it's not to your taste, you can choose something different."

The little box was still tucked into her hand. She gave it a tilt, and the low light reflected back to her from many facets of a square-cut diamond in a shapely, platinum band. "It's beautiful, Hank." With shaking fingers, she lifted it out of the little box and slid it onto the third finger of her left hand. When she held out her hand to look, it winked back at her, a dazzling bit of light that she wasn't sure she'd ever see on her otherwise-unadorned hand. "I don't…I haven't ever sat around thinking about how engagement rings ought to look. You chose it for me, so it's perfect."

He gave a little growl into her ear and kissed her neck. "So are you." His arms closed around her waist. "I found the very best girl, and now I've tricked her into saying yes."

Callie smiled down at her ring. "I didn't know you wanted to get married. You never brought it up." Even after the beautiful year they'd just shared, her heart whispered doubts to her sometimes. She hoped the proposal wasn't an impulse he'd regret later.

"I like to shoot first and ask questions later, Callie. If you said no, or said you weren't sure, I figured we'd talk about it then. I could try to change your mind."

"Risky," Callie teased, nuzzling him. His unusual silence made sense now. "You were *nervous*. And here I thought you were fearless."

"Naw," Hank chuckled. "Everybody gets nervous. It's just that I don't let it stop me."

"Pssst!" Willow cleared her throat. "Can I see that ring, yet? I'm dying, here." Callie reached back to put her hand over the back of the seat. "Oooh! It's so *you*, Callie. Classy."

"Okay, she's invited to the wedding," Hank said.

Little Finley climbed over to see what all the fuss was about. "Pretty!" she said, petting the blue velvet box.

"Isn't there a party we're supposed to be attending now?" Callie asked, sliding off Hank's lap.

"If we have to," Hank said. Then he dropped his voice. "I'd prefer a more private celebration."

"But I do feel like having a glass of champagne." She picked up her purse, and went to fetch Hank's wheelchair.

When she returned, Dane was shaking Hank's hand. And then he took a step back and began scanning the upper corners of the entire room, near the ceiling.

"Dane, what are you doing?" Willow asked.

"Checking for flying pigs. You don't want to be standing under one of those suckers when it lets loose."

"Stop, asshole," Hank snorted.

But his protests were drowned out by laughter. The others moved toward the exit, but Callie hung back as Hank sat in his chair. When they were alone, she made herself comfortable on his lap for a moment. "What kind of a wedding do you want to have?" she asked. She had visions of an old Vermont inn, during leaf season.

"I'm a guy. We don't care about that shit," Hank confessed. "As long as it involves you in a skimpy dress, booze and a nice trip somewhere, I'm good."

"So you've given it a lot of thought," Callie deadpanned.

He laughed. "Have you?"

"Not ever. I'm *still* surprised. And I'm not the only one who was," she said, hugging him.

"But you're the only one who counts," he whispered. "I mean it, Callie. It's been a great year. Every day I love you more."

Her heart was bursting. "I love you, too, Hazardous." And she leaned in to kiss him.

The
End

ABOUT THE AUTHOR

Sarina Bowen lives in snowy New England, where her hardier ancestors first began farming and logging 250 years ago. She appreciates soft cheese, hard cider and powder days. Sarina lives with her ski-crazy husband, two sons and eight chickens. Visit her at www.sarinabowen.com.

Visit Sarina:
www.sarinabowen.com

Made in the USA
Middletown, DE
02 December 2023

44349817R00144